Frozen to the Core

Best Wishes

Paul Cude

ISBN-13: 978-1709051142

FROZEN TO THE CORE

A haze of brilliant, bright, white light haunted him, even in his dream state. It was inescapable and all he'd ever known.

"Man, Man... wake up, we're late," echoed a husky voice, as dirty nails on the end of emaciated fingers dug in, attempting to shake him awake.

Mirroring every single day of his life so far, pain flooded his very essence, startling every atom of his body into life. It was all he could do not to cry out, but he'd learnt the hard way, long, long ago that that really wasn't an option. A wave of numbing, ice cold needles washed over him as he tried to peel his lips apart with his tongue, his eyes still closed.

"Man, Man... come on, we have to go!"

Applying all of his considerable will, he commanded the muscles in his arms, legs and back to move, ignoring the excruciating agony coursing through him.

"Alright, I'm coming," he uttered, his breath freezing in front of his face, something so commonplace there that no one would give it even a second thought.

"We're so late," reflected Josh. "Boy are we gonna get it!"

"I've already told you Josh... I'm coming. And don't worry, it'll be alright. We won't get into trouble."

"How can you say that? You know how they can be."

"I'll deal with it, alright?"

"What about if we skipped feeding him? Missing one meal wouldn't hurt and that way we'll be on time for lessons."

Ragged scraps of clothing tore huge slivers of frost off the makeshift block of chilly ice that he slept on, night after night, as he bounded to his feet, standing nose to nose with his brother Josh.

"What have I told you? He's our responsibility. If

something happens to him, it's on us," admonished Man, quietly.

"But if we go and feed him now, we'll be late and you know the consequences when that happens," emphasised Josh anxiously.

"I do. But I also know about responsibility and so do you. Let's go feed him, and scoot off straight away to join the others. Don't forget... we're important to them... a new generation if you will. They regard us as such and are constantly saying it. So believe it! They need us more than ever, particularly if we're going to leave this place."

Nodding in agreement at his sibling's wise words, Josh knew his brother was right. It was just that they scared him, and more than a little. At that exact moment, a huge smile broke out across Man's smooth jaw, the chill of their surroundings forgotten momentarily, along with the others and any punishment that might be forthcoming. After punching each other playfully, and with all the grip they could muster on the slippery, cold, reflective surface they found themselves on, both shot off at speed around the corner, determined to fulfil their duties to the best of their abilities and live up to their responsibilities, no matter what the cost.

In a small, walled off, icy chamber about a mile away, in another part of the strength sapping prison, rage, anger and fury bubbled dangerously to the surface. A one hundred and eighty degree roundhouse kick, followed swiftly by a sharp punch splintered a delicate formation of stalactites into a thousand pieces. A roar of immense frustration accompanied the act.

"Aaarrrrghhhh..." reverberated off the walls.

"Feel better now?" asked a ragged male voice.

"Not really."

"What a surprise! Surely there must be a better way?"

"And just what would that be?

"Honestly, I don't know. I just hate seeing you like this," stated his second in command.

"Don't you think I hate it too? The way this damn cold suppresses everything that we are frustrates the hell out of me, even after all these years. Every time I delve inside myself, I can feel it there... the tiniest of sparks, frantically zipping about, always just out of reach. I can't tell you how many times each and every day I reach out to try and capture it, always to be denied. I know that if I can grasp that tiny inkling, then it will all come rushing back and I will be as powerful again as I once was."

Downcast, the other face in the room soaked up all the words.

"Don't you think it's like that for all of us? Everyone here does exactly the same thing, probably on a minute by minute basis, with the same degree of success as you have. They took it away from all of us, and I hope one day to make them pay dearly. But I know that day is a long way off. Because of your plan though, we at least have a smidgen of hope, even if we do have to bide our time."

The cool, calculating dragon stuck in a depressingly dull human form listened to his friend's words of encouragement, briefly buoyed by what he had to say.

The plan... that was all they had. It was that, or nothing. Those superior idiots assumed they'd thought of everything, assumed they'd be contained, controlled, deemed no threat whatsoever and that they would eventually die in this frosty hellhole. Boy was he going to prove them wrong. Of course it might take decades, centuries even, but one way or another he would have his revenge, and when he did, the world itself would pay dearly for their incarceration.

Panting heavily, the brothers, Man and Josh, slid to a halt alongside one of the row of magically contained hydroponics bays. Ten metres by ten metres, a dazzling sparkle encompassed the entire circumference, a warm, yellow glow threatening to seep through from the inside. But it never did. Standing up straight, their hands clasped together behind the back of their heads, desperately trying to pull in a deep breath despite the pain that accompanied it, the two of them stood admiring the supernatural miracle in front of them that was filled to the brim with vegetables. Beetroot, beans, broccoli, cabbage cauliflowers, carrots, peppers, cucumbers, leeks and lettuce were just a small sample of what was being grown in this particular section of this underground, frozen domain. In all honesty, it was an absolute marvel, one immensely complicated to pull off, and one not of their making. And unfortunately for everyone there, it worked flawlessly as designed and had no scope for alteration or tampering... goodness knows the best of them there had tried, all to no avail. You see, the mantras used to provide the heat for the soil within were designed to recognise a pulse or heartbeat of any sort. The moment one enters the area of heat generation, immediately the powerful magic cuts out, thus denying any of the beings there a fleeting taste of the warmth they all so long for. Despite being awed by the cleverness of the power sustaining them all, to Man and his brother it was just one more reminder of the injustice they rallied against, and the cruelty of their long gone jailers. Both of them found it best not dwelt upon.

Without hesitation, both grabbed a sack from a pile on the floor nearby, and stepping onto the fertile earth, began gathering as much as they could each carry. Instantly the warm yellow glow disappeared as the magic kicked in, the cool of the surroundings rushing to fill the tiny space. In the matter of minutes that it had taken the brothers to fill their sacks, frost had started to appear on greenery, forming tiny little icy pockets between the undulations of the earth. Understanding the need to be swift, the two of them scurried out across the dirt, a sense of relief washing over them as the heat from the magic resumed. Although they couldn't touch or feel it, it felt good to know that it was there, both could agree on that. Sacks slung over their shoulders, the two of them followed the winding path that meandered up and over a slippery rise, before cutting down at quite an angle beside a rocky wall. The sound of gurgling water told them that they were close. Struggling to stay on their feet, the two rounded a cold and treacherous corner, finally reaching their destination.

Curled into an almost perfect spiral, a brown scaled appendage with just a hint of dark green, the caudal spade (the tip of the dragon's tail) resting perfectly on top, was the first things the brothers noticed.

"Ahhhhhhh... so nice of both of you to join me. I was beginning to wonder if I'd be fed at all today."

Rising up from an icy shelf below the level of his tail, an elegant, slightly brow beaten and undernourished dragon body appeared, as if from nowhere. The tinkling rattle of chains accompanied his movement.

"We always turn up, don't we?" announced Man, cheerfully.

"I suppose you do, I suppose you do," thundered the dragon.

"I should count yourself lucky if I were you. You get ten times more than any of us," scoffed Josh, unhappy at how his day had started.

"Yes... I can see how that would be some sort of burden. I have asked numerous times to be put out of my misery. All of my requests so far have been flatly ignored."

"You don't want that... not really," cajoled Man.

"On the contrary, I want nothing else. The cold tortures me with such mind numbing pain, every second of every day, that death would be a welcome release. These chains and the temperatures prevent me from doing it myself. Perhaps you'd care to oblige?"

"I'd do it in a heartbeat," bragged Josh, taking two steps forward.

Man held out his arm to stop the brother he loved.

"Nobody's doing anything like that," he announced. "This is all rather depressing for the start of a brand new day. Why don't you let us show you what we've bought you?"

"As you wish," replied the dragon, one of its huge prehistoric eyes constantly focused on the threat one of the two brothers posed.

Crunching across the ice, both of them came to a jagged line of rocks, jutting out from the ground. Careful not to move beyond them and into the dragon's reach, they threw the contents of their shabby sacks in the direction of the prehistoric beast.

"Still no meat... I'm stunned," observed the beast, its mighty neck bent over on itself in an effort to inspect the contents of its latest meal.

"At least you know what meat tastes like," fumed Josh, his ire starting to rise.

"Enough!" commanded Man, much to his brother's displeasure. "It's not his fault. Just like us, he's stuck here as well, and so we've all got to make the best of a very bad situation."

'Wise words indeed,' thought the dragon, having enough common sense not to say it out loud, lest he antagonise the younger of the two any more than he already had.

About ready to turn and walk away, their first chore of the day completed, it was then that Man spotted something unusual.

"You seem to have hurt yourself. How'd you do that?" he asked.

Running down his arched, scaled back, two diagonal lines of dripping, dried green blood glistened in the brightness of the only stuttering electric light in this whole section. The wounds looked beyond painful, and most certainly hadn't been there yesterday.

Straightening up and unfurling his well muscled tail, the dragon stood as tall as the chains would allow to address the two beings in front of him.

"It's nothing... only a consequence of falling asleep on the ice. It must have torn the scales off when I awoke and stood up this morning. So inconsequential that I didn't even notice... that's the cold for you."

The way in which the words were said was upbeat, or about as upbeat as it got around here. But there was something else, something very wrong, or at least that was Man's instinctive reaction. But what could it be? Having been squirreled away in the icy confines of this tortuous prison since his birth, he had very little real world experience to draw on, making him, like his brother, unbelievably naive. Spotting a lie for him was much like sighting the Loch Ness monster. You had a sneaking suspicion that it was there, but until it reared its ugly head and was pointed out by someone else that that's what it was, there was just simply no way for either of the brothers to recognise it. That was something that would change much later on. And so with a strange niggling feeling eating away at the pit of his stomach, Man turned on his heels, along with Josh, leaving the dragon to his vegetarian diet, the upshot of which could be heard resounding in and out of the rock formation he was chained to, for the next few minutes. Dragons really were meant to be carnivores, something the noses of every being incarcerated there could surely attest to.

It was shoddy, unkempt, filthy and of course, devastatingly cold, but it was all that they had as a community. Over the course of a decade, intense manual labour had been used to carve out what could only be described as an amphitheatre. Glistening white mounds of frozen water had been carved into level, semicircular benches, in rows that fed up the sloping mound on which the construction of epic proportions sat. It truly was a marvel. Directly at the front lay a smooth circle of stone in the middle of which lay a plinth made of rock. Currently a thin, frail, old, white haired human shape stood beside the pedestal, addressing sixteen or so much younger denizens dotted about the different tiers of the amphitheatre. The subject of discussion was that of harnessing a being's own innate magical ability, and calling forth the power from deep within a physical body. Of course, it was all theoretical at the moment, because being constantly subjected to these kind of temperatures wouldn't allow even the most formidable amongst them to access what was rightfully theirs, something the very disappointed and angry leader could attest to. Hypothetical was all they had left, but all was not lost. Everything did, however, rest on the plan blooming into fruition. Luck needed to play its part. If it didn't, they'd be stuck here for all time.

With the kind of stealth and precision normally only associated with ninjas, two pairs of eyes peeped out from the end of one empty tier of the amphitheatre. Taking note of the impromptu teacher's positioning, they waited patiently for him to turn in the opposite direction. When he did, Man and Josh slid silently out into the tier, the tatty rags covering their bottoms sliding seamlessly and silently to a halt on one of the glossy, white benches about a quarter of the way in. Exhaling a sigh of relief at having arrived unnoticed, the small moment of joy was quickly and very publically quelled.

"WELL... IF IT IS'NT OUR FITTEST AND FINEST! HOW FANTASTIC OF YOU TO JOIN US. I THINK I CAN SPEAK FOR ALL OF US AND SAY THAT WE FEEL WELL AND TRULY HONOURED!"

Josh quaked uncontrollably, while Man just shook his head. This wasn't how it was supposed to go.

"So which one of you would like to come down to the front and explain some of these principles to those among us that have deigned to turn up on time?"

Josh's hands were a blur, they were quivering so hard. Man's choice had already been made for him. He'd always stand up for his younger brother, of that there was no doubt. And so with a confidence that hid how truly terrified he really was, he jumped to his feet, and announced cockily,

"I will!"

With all eyes on him, Man negotiated the tricky, sloping stairs and walkways, quickly arriving at the plinth next to the still glaring teacher, a being by the name of Meeks, who was renowned for having a quick and vicious temper.

"So boy... what have you got to say for yourself?"

Although relatively naive, as previously mentioned, Man recognised a trap when he saw one, and remembering a student having been hurled halfway across the auditorium less than a week ago, by this very same being, from a blistering punch that had come out of nowhere after a wrong answer had been given, he very sensibly chose to remain silent, something he hoped would serve him well.

"Basilisk got your tongue?"

Readying for anything that might come his way, he remained silent.

"Very well then... we shall continue where we left off. Before we were so rudely interrupted, our topic had been..."

Meeks left it hanging in the air.

"Recognising, and bringing forth the power of our birthright!" one student sat up high, shouted out.

"Precisely!" praised Meeks, much to the particular scholar's glee.

'Suck-up,' Man thought, glad telepathy was cancelled out by the chilly environment.

"And so perhaps you could give us your thoughts on the subject young man? Deeming to turn up so late, you must of course already know everything pertaining to the subject at hand."

'Here we go,' he thought.

And so the apparently weak, frail old man stood there

in silence, piling on the pressure, determined to show up this upstart for what he was in front of his peers. From on high, Josh cringed at seeing his brother in this precarious position.

The tiniest bead of sweat rolled down the side of Man's neck, no mean feat in the icy hellhole they found themselves cooped up in. Struggling to think of a strategy, or even a lie to save a little face, Josh's brother fell back on the only thing he could think of, the very last thing a politician would trust in. The truth!

Despite the adults all thinking him a no good waster, but having to be careful about saying exactly that because of just who his father was, in fact he was a quick and studious learner. Although appearing on many an occasion not to have paid attention at any of the right times, nothing could be further from the truth. A desire to learn and constantly improve was ingrained in his very DNA, which was more than could be said of his brother, who had to be helped and prompted in most of the work that they participated in.

Closing his eyes, ignoring those all around him, he sought out the memory of those illicit late night practices that nobody else knew about but him. Lying there, pushing the devastating cold off to one side, he would centre his mind, slow his heart and delve deep within himself. Time passed slowly, his breathing reducing to almost nothing. Pinpricks of cold stabbed at his exposed flesh, determined to waylay his focus. But he'd almost found the solace he was looking for, and continued on unperturbed. It wasn't the first time he'd tried this, but on no other occasion had he got this far. And then out of the blue... it was there, almost within touching distance. A blazing blue, purple and green perfectly spherical ball of what looked like fire, but was clearly ethereal energy, danced before him, calling to him, tempting him, offering up itself completely. Totally mesmerised at first, he just studied it intently, a mixture of pleasure and relief running through him. They'd been told magic would be theirs, that the creative way they'd sidestepped their captors' objectives would work, and that they would be the key to escaping this unforgiving confinement. And so it proved to be, there and then there could be no doubt. Over time, he'd discovered how to access it, and despite knowing that it was forbidden, had come to use it, even in the bone chilling temperatures that surrounded them all, something he was pretty sure no other being there could do. It was both exhilarating and frightening and something he kept completely under wraps, even from his brother.

Snapping back to reality, he pushed away the wave of ecstasy he experienced at just the thought of his magic, and feeling much more sure of himself, described in detail his very first encounter with his rightful power, right down to the colours and shape of the magic, sure not to give anything away about exactly what he'd been up to.

The other students sat, mouths agog. Josh's eyes were as wide as they could possibly go. Meeks disguised his surprise at the accuracy of his words, well, for the most part anyway.

"Not bad," ventured the spindly looking teacher. "Tell me about how you use it!"

A quandary couldn't begin to describe Man's situation. Wondering what he should do, a booming voice added considerably to the proceedings, and Man's dilemma.

"I AGREE WHOLEHEARTEDLY! TELL US ALL ABOUT HOW YOU USE YOUR MAGIC!"

Instantly recognising his father's voice, fear ran riot throughout his body, causing his legs to wobble, his arms to shake, his stomach to roll and his mind to fold back in on itself. His father had always had that kind of effect on him.

High up in the tiers of the amphitheatre, Josh slunk down low, even more afraid than Man of the being that had spawned him. Even though he'd done everything and more to try and please his dad, nothing had ever come close to working. Not once had any love, or even a touch of kindness passed between the two of them. For all intents and purposes, they were total strangers, not related at all. But he was sure that would change, when or if he could conjure up any sort of magic. After all, that's what he'd been born into this world for. That had been the plan. If he could achieve and master that, he was sure he could gain the love and trust of his father.

"WELL...?"

His thoughts were a muddle, his mind a mess. The truth felt fraudulent and so far away. Feeling the penetrating stare of his father piercing him to the very core of his being, he decided to come clean.

"I've been able to access it on occasions to heal minor injuries and..."

It was this bit that he was afraid of revealing.

"...to keep me warm."

A collective intake of sighs whistled around the auditorium.

"WHAT?!"

Man's nervousness seemed to have surpassed that of a chicken walking through a KFC car park.

"I...I...I...I managed to use it to keep me warm, only once or twice though."

"I SEE. AND YOU THINK THAT MAKES IT OKAY NOT TO TELL US? NOT TO TELL ME?"

It was at that point he made the mistake of looking over at his father, instantly noticing the crazy look in his eyes. Quickly he averted his gaze. At some point there would be hell to pay, he knew.

Strolling out next to the plinth from his previous position on the sidelines, the de facto leader of this tiny, stranded community, and father to two, addressed everyone there, his voice a little more calm and rational.

"So there it is... the reason you're all here. If one of you can do it, doubtless there will be more. An extraordinary amount of time and resources have gone into your creation. Sacrifices have been made by everybody."

A rising anger deep inside Man threatened to spill out on hearing these words leave his father's lips.

"Slowly though, everything is coming to fruition. Use this as an example. Spend every minute of every hour of your free time searching for that ethereal spark. Nurture it, reassure it, tame it, and ultimately use it. The one thing you should NOT do is hide it."

With a very obvious dig at his son and the tiniest hint of the punishment he could expect, the rest of the words were spat out with more than a hint of anger and frustration.

"If we find out that you've been pulling the wool over our eyes with regard to this, there will be dire consequences for all of you. We need to work together if we're ever to escape and make our way back to the real world. It will take each and every one of us, particularly those that can wield any sort of magical power in this hideous environment. Now go... forgo any work or lessons that you had for the rest of the day. Meditate, relax and concentrate on finding that which we need from each of you, if we're ever likely to escape."

As one, the students got up and left, glad to be out from under the watchful eye of their fearsome leader. Only one remained, hidden behind a frost rimmed balcony, too afraid to stick his head out to see what was going on.

"So my son, you like to keep secrets?"

"N...n...n...not... a...a...at all," Man managed to stutter.

"That's not how it seems."

Swallowing nervously, all he could think to do was remain silent.

Even Meeks was getting nervous now, constantly hopping from foot to foot.

"Did it never occur to you that I would need to know about the use of your power? You know about the plan, how long it's taken to get to this point, the struggles, the hardship, the toll it's taken on all of us."

'Some more than others,' thought the youngster, not daring to say it out loud.

A short way away, Josh had exactly the same thought.

"Ahhh... thoughts turning to your mother?" goaded Man's father, right on the button. "How is she? Surviving I hope."

A cold day in hell would be the day he talked to his father about his mother.

"Anyhow, no more secrets! As a community we need to know. And I will be testing the extent of your powers from tomorrow onwards," he said, the words sounding kinder and much more melodic now. "Have you worked out how to unlock the bonds of your DNA and reach the beast within you? Be honest now!"

"No!" Man replied instantly, having not gotten anywhere near doing so, despite trying.

Believing every word, the group's leader took a step in the direction of his son, as pride engulfed his weatherworn face. For the briefest of instants, Man's heart sang. It lasted about a thousandth of a second. A wave of cold air rushing over his face was his first clue. By then, he was out of time. A resounding 'CRACK' echoed around the amphitheatre as Man's nose split in two from the powerful uppercut his dad had unleashed.

Up high, tears attempted to flow down Josh's cheeks. He didn't even need to see what had happened. It was all so obvious and predictable.

Using all his strength and willpower, Man stayed on his feet, albeit more than a little unsteady.

"USE YOUR MAGIC TO FIX THAT!" fumed his father, before turning on his heels and striding purposefully away.

As thick, crimson blood ran freely across his lips, down his chin and pooled precariously on the floor, all he could think of was his mother, and everything the poor woman had been through at the hands of that monster.

Too conflicted to be able to use the tiny spark of power within him to heal the damage to his nose, on the walk back from the amphitheatre Man had settled for applying fistfuls of ice to it as he walked along. That hurt almost as much as the initial injury itself. At the intersection up ahead where two of the slippery, bright paths met, Man could just make out his brother's form, waiting patiently for him. Forgoing the usual fist bump greeting, Josh inspected the harm inflicted on his sibling.

"I'm sorry. Are you okay? Is there anything I can do?"

"No it's okay. It'll be fine in a while," Man replied, all bunged up and nasal.

"It should have been me," Josh confessed. "Once again you've stepped in to protect me. It's not right. You should have let it be me."

"What are big brothers for, if not exactly that?" Man smiled. "Besides, it's in the past now. Let's just forget it and move on."

And so they did, at least to some degree, moving off in the same direction, up a slight incline, heading off in the direction of the female quarters some ten or fifteen minutes walk away.

After a short pause, Josh broke the uncomfortable silence.

"Did you mean what you said? Can you access your magic and can it keep you warm?"

"It's true, I can."

"Why didn't you tell me? I'd have been absolutely elated for you."

"I know you would have been. But there's more to it than that. I thought at first that it was a one off fluke. It took an absolute age to do it again and even then I wasn't sure. And when I said to Father that I could use the power to keep myself warm... well, I did, only once and it didn't work particularly well. In fact it was more than a little pathetic and not something anyone would want to brag about. So that's why... I was more ashamed at not being able to do fantastical things with it, than proud to have found it at all."

"But just think," continued Josh, "you can use your magic here, where no one else can. Think of the potential, think of the power you must have if that's an option. That must be why Father was so upset."

"Agreed."

They, like all of the other youngsters, had all heard about their father, and exactly how powerful he'd been in his previous life. And from the sound of it, more powerful than almost any other being on the planet, or at least that's how it had been made to seem. Most of them here were in awe of his father and bowed down and kowtowed to their demanding leader, including all of the brothers' peers. But in Man's mind, all these tales raised more questions than answers. If he'd been so powerful, how had he and his followers ended up here? That didn't sound like something that could or should happen to one of the most powerful beings on the planet. And if he had that much magic, how was it possible that the cold here could keep it at bay? Surely he must have been able to produce some remnant of power, however insignificant? And just what made him think this new generation could call forth their magic, when none of the others here could? It was all very odd, and almost always set alarm bells ringing in his head when any of these stories were mentioned.

Twenty minutes later, out of breath and with the blood from his nose finally having stopped running, they reached a carefully sculpted arch beneath an icy overhang that had stalactites raining down from it. Beautiful to look at, to all who sheltered behind these walls it was just one more reminder of their incarceration and the terrible toll it was taking on them.

As the boys took two paces forward, from out of the shadow stepped a haggard, brown haired woman wearing the remains of a dirty old sack, ice caking her legs and one side of her face, looking incredibly put down and despondent.

"Oh... it's the two of you. I suppose you can go in."

"Thank you," the brothers uttered, eager to get away.

Before they could, the browbeaten woman continued.

"They're still doing it, you know. It's supposed to have stopped."

Instantly they froze, and not because of the cold this time. Of course they knew what she was going on about, but it really wasn't wise to talk about it, not here, not anywhere.

"He came for your mother again, you know!"

This got their attention.

"When?" demanded Man, fury coursing through his veins, his voice much harsher than he'd meant it to be.

Taking a small step back in fright, the now scared woman locked eyes with Man before replying.

"Last night. She was brought back this morning."

Man shook his head, closed his eyes and tried to ignore the pulsing pain from his nose.

"Thank you," he whispered softly, nodding graciously towards the woman as he did so.

"I'm so sorry," she ventured, her teeth by now chattering in the cold.

"So are we, so are we," replied Man, making his way past her, ducking under the archway, followed closely by Josh, the two of them disappearing deep within the labyrinth of twisted tunnels that made up this part of the chilling prison they all found themselves trapped in.

As they followed their usual path in total silence, on their way to see their mother, both of them barely contained the rage and vehemence they felt. The atrocious acts that had been committed in the past in the name of the long term plan, were, unbelievably, still going on. It was impossible to see how that could still be happening. It should have all stopped, long ago. Both of their hearts threatened to break at the thought of what their mother, and no doubt the rest of the women, were still enduring.

Two sharp left hand turns and a one hundred and eighty degree right hand turn later, they arrived at the stupendously small space that had been designated as their mother's. Lying in the harsh, cold and damp corner, their mother shivered as she slept, curled up in the foetal position, wheezing occasionally as her ragged breath went in and out. It was all the boys could do not to cry.

Almost right on cue, whatever nightmare she was suffering from seemed to get worse, forcing her to cry out in pain, screaming, "No... no... no!" at the top of her voice. Both boys rushed over, just as she came around.

"Mother," they both exclaimed.

"Oh boys... it's so good to see you."

As gently as they could, they helped their mother to her feet, brushing a little of the ice off her as they did so. As she stood, they both noticed the bruising on her legs and wrists. A bitter resentment threatened to send them both over the edge. Clearly clued into her sons' feelings, their mother tried to dismiss it all.

"It's okay. It's just one of those things. It'll stop soon."

"IT'S NOT OKAY UNDER ANY CIRCUMSTANCES!" growled a furious Man.

"He's right," added his brother softly.

"Boys... please, let it go."

Sensing there was nowhere else to go, and not wanting to upset their mother further, both brothers let it drop, for now at least.

"So what's your day been like?" their mother asked.

"Man's found his magic and has even been able to use it," blurted out Josh excitedly.

"Really?" exclaimed their mother.

Deeply ashamed for the most part, Man really didn't want to get into all of it at the moment, and gave his brother a withering look for spilling the beans so to speak. Try as he might though, he wasn't going to disappoint his mum by not sharing the details with her, now they were out in the open. She and Josh were the two beings on the whole of the planet that he trusted and loved the most.

And so after they'd all sat down and made themselves as comfortable as possible, he told her everything. To say she was surprised was something of an understatement. Pride radiated off her like rays from the sun, something that cheered him up considerably. As well, all talk of magic and using it to push away the cold, did at least distract from the pain and heartache that she was suffering from, something Man was incredibly grateful for.

After munching their way through a few raw vegetables and sipping fresh, ice cold water from the rusty metal cups that had been left here for them to use at the time of their confinement, their thoughts turned to what would happen next.

"The plan actually seems to be working, at least the first part anyway," ventured their mother.

Man sat hunched forward, head in hands, trying to wrap his mind around everything that had happened.

"And what of you Scooter? How are you feeling about all of this?"

Scooter was her nickname for Josh and something she'd called him since he'd scooted around on the ice as an enthusiastic toddler.

As his mother was one of the two beings he felt he could be totally honest with, Josh relayed his fears.

"I'm scared that I won't be able to find my power, or that I won't have any at all. What if that happens? I'll just be a burden, taking up more of our limited resources, unable to contribute in any meaningful way. I'm not sure what Father would do if that were the case."

"It won't come to that... rest assured I'll see to it personally," declared Man.

"Thanks," replied Josh, "but don't make promises that you probably can't keep. It doesn't befit you."

"Oh I'll keep it alright. If they want me to use my magic to help them, then you can be damn sure it's going to come at a price. And that price will always be the safety and wellbeing of my family... both of you!"

It was at that point it all got too much. All three of them hugged, glistening teardrops spewing from their eyes, each one freezing before reaching the bottom of their faces. Crying in temperatures like this was ill advised. After long goodbyes, the two boys left the women's section, heading back to their squared off bunks. Neither said a word, until they both had to go their separate ways.

"Thanks," stated Josh, proffering out his hand.

Man took it and pulled him in tight.

"You don't owe me your thanks. Always being there and just being my brother is enough. Always together, never apart."

"Always together, never apart," repeated Josh. "I love you, you know."

"I know," replied Man with a smile. "I love you too. Now go and get some rest, and perhaps we won't be late for anything tomorrow."

Josh smiled, turned and headed off in the direction of his own tiny space.

Man stood stock still for a few moments yet, a steely gaze imprinted on his face. Those two beings were all that he cared about, all that he had. And he'd be damned if anything more would harm or endanger them. Having always been afraid to stand up to his father, one thing here and now became plainly obvious. The time was near at hand when he'd have to. And he'd be ready. If need be, he might even be prepared to use that ethereal spark of power that he now knew resided within him. It was ironic that he'd told his brother to get some rest, because he had no intention of sleeping. Instead, he'd be searching for his power, caressing it, exploring its boundaries, willing it to do his bidding, all in an effort to keep those that he loved safe. In only a matter of minutes, he was tucked away, lying on his own block of ice.

The next morning, Josh appeared earlier than the previous day, only to find, unusually, his brother up and about, having already bathed in the communal ice cold pool that resided nearby, also having washed his straggly hair, something they all avoided, right until the very last minute anyway.

Heading off in good time to find the first meal of the day for the captive dragon they thought of as 'Unlucky', before they even had a chance to leave Man's portion of the youth development wing, three hulking great guards appeared, stopping them in their tracks. The two siblings stood there, facing off, tiny flakes of ice floating around in the air between them, Josh a step behind his brother.

"You're to come with us," issued the biggest of the three to Man.

"Why?" asked the elder of the two brothers.

"Because our leader demands it, and that should be enough."

Resigned to having no choice, Man took a step forward to accompany the guards. Josh clutched at his arm.

"It's okay. Go and feed him like normal, and then get off to lessons. I'll see you later on."

"I'm...I'm...I'm scared. What's he going to do to you?"

"Nothing, if he knows what's good for him. It'll be fine. I'll come and find you later."

And with that, Man turned and, flanked by the three hulking great individuals, headed off in the direction of the leader's accommodation.

Joy personified, that's how it felt as the shatteringly cold water whipped through his gills, oxygenating his body, filling him with physical energy, spurring him on to glide through the water even faster in an effort to keep up with his prey. Normally two or three of his kind would group together in an effort to take down a beast like this, but not today. On his own, with the community having been afforded some time to themselves, they'd agreed to convene again in no more than another week. What he had for once, was time, which he'd chosen to spend exploring, and in doing so had come across something his kind thought of as a delicacy. So here he was, propelling himself forward with everything he had, in the wake of a five metre long orca (killer whale to you and me), its huge black body, white underbelly and white patch above and behind its eyes barely visible through the turbulent, bitterly cold water. Of course he had taken out a number of these intelligent and highly evolved creatures before, but only in a group of his peers. This was the first time he'd attempted to do it alone, and it was much, much harder than he had thought it would be. The orca had been outrunning him for nearly an hour now, using all the tricks it knew to try and shake him off its tail. So far to no avail, but exhaustion was threatening his hand. If he didn't take the beast down in the next few minutes, then the battle would be well and truly over before it began, and that just wouldn't do. Nobody would hear about it, of that he was sure. Who on earth could be around in this particular part of the Antarctic, from his race, to see the potential failure? NO ONE! But his pride and family heritage demanded that he didn't fail, and so he gave one last push in an effort to catch up with the monstrous mammal.

Through all of her twisting and turning, and the panic of an unknown predator chasing her down, the orca, a pregnant female, began to suffer from fatigue and instead of swimming out into the open ocean, she opted to head towards land in the hope that she could somehow shake off the terrifying looking creature hunting her down. Knowing the shelves and precarious underwater ice formations of this particular region well, she was confident she could lose her pursuer, if only tiredness didn't overtake her.

For her shadow, things were becoming desperate. So

much so, that he'd almost reverted to using the ancient magic that coursed so freely throughout his snake-like body... almost, but not quite. It would have been, as far as he was concerned, bad form to say the least. His skill and prowess as a hunter should have been enough to see him capture and devour this monster of the seas entirely on his own. To use his ethereal gift would have been nothing short of cheating, and that wasn't something he wanted to taste when he eventually polished off the mother of all snacks. Snaking this way and that, lithe as a torpedo, he followed the desperate mother-to-be, noticing for the first time the slightest of bulges in her stomach.

'She's pregnant,' he thought only to himself.

Did it make a difference to the chase? Barely! But somewhere deep inside his subconscious, a switch had been flicked, the tiredness he fought forcing him to slow just a little, allowing the gap between the two of them to open out a touch. A thought came to him completely out of nowhere.

'Do you actually need to eat? Are you even hungry?'

Distracting him momentarily, he knew the answer to both questions. NO! Don't need to eat. Not hungry. But that wasn't the point, was it? The hunt was everything, at least that's what he'd been taught all those years ago. But he was an individual, not anyone's puppet, and so gliding gracefully to a halt beside a huge underwater ice formation, he knowingly and gladly gave up the chase, wishing the orca well from a distance.

Chasing his tail for a few moments, before swimming alongside the mountainous wall of subterranean ice a few metres below the water's surface, he noticed a dark foreboding opening, disappearing off in the direction of the snow covered landmass. He took mere moments to decide, as he'd always been inquisitive, a side to him that nothing and no one could contain. So without a thought for his own safety, and nothing but wonderment in his mind at what lay ahead, he dived head first through the gap and kicked his tail out to gain as much momentum as possible. As far as he was concerned, the adventure had well and truly begun.

Rounding a dark, sharp, left hand corner, the three guards stopped where they were, one of them indicating to Man with his outstretched arm that he should proceed without them. He did. It wasn't the first time that he'd been in his father's icy chambers, not by a long stretch, but it had been some time since his last visit. As youngsters, he and Josh had spent many an hour playing in the bedecked billet. Although he couldn't describe those memories as happy, he did miss that time in his life. Everything had seemed so much simpler. There was no right or wrong, no politics, no plan, no magic and the anger, resentment, frustration and fury of this place, seemed not to have existed. Of course he was mistaken. It had always been this way, from the second they'd been trapped here, but because of his age and naivety, he'd just not been aware of it.

Perched on an actual chair made up from an assortment of different pieces of scrap wood, his father, the community's leader, sat off to one side of the room, carefully running his fingers over a tiny rock formation ingrained in the wall, choosing not to look in his direction as he entered the room.

'So it's going to be like that,' thought Man, knowing that he was not getting off to a great start.

Standing to attention, Man waited for his father to say something. It took a while.

Finally the leader deigned to look in his son's direction.

"Nice of you to join me."

"Was there a choice?"

"I suppose you think you're clever?"

Man knew that if it looked like a trap and felt like a trap, then almost certainly it was a trap. He remained silent.

"You seem to have developed quite a high opinion of yourself around here. Showing up for lessons late, if at all, hiding the abilities that we've granted you... It doesn't paint a particularly good picture, does it?"

There was only one being there that had an overinflated opinion of himself, Man knew, and he was standing directly opposite him. An overwhelming sense of danger and fear continued to keep him quiet.

"The future of every being held against their will here could depend on your actions, even the very planet itself, and you still continue to play these games," his father continued.

'The only one playing games is you,' thought Man, wondering where the hell this was all going.

"Your cooperation is mandatory. Don't think otherwise. If we need to, we can take what we want from you. It won't be pleasant, but I'm sure it will be possible," his father gloated. "And then there's the matter of your mother and sibling. It would be a crying shame if anything untoward were to happen to them. Accidents, as you know, are commonplace in this unforgiving environment... a stray fall here, a catastrophic rock slide there. Fate can prove to be both fickle and unpredictable. It would be terrible if they were to succumb to something so callous."

For the first time ever, he couldn't feel the cold because a piercing hot rage filling all of his extremities, burning away any hint of a chill, threatened to break down any barriers of commonsense and self preservation Man had erected. Only thoughts of his brother and mother kept him on the straight and narrow and away from the spark of magic he knew he could conjure up at any time. Thoughts of doing so intertwined with his body, but that tiny little voice we all have screamed at him that it might not be enough.

"Remember," it said, "just how powerful an opponent he is supposed to be. Recall the stories. They'd been backed up by so many of the others, that there must be something to them. Take care!" And so he did, just standing there, staring straight ahead, giving no outward sign that any of the words had affected him, in a show of complete and utter defiance, at least that's how he saw it. His father had a totally different take on things, sure that his son had come around to his way of thinking.

Two worlds on totally different paths which would collide at some point in the not too distant future.

It had started off as a bit of fun, an adventure. On entering the cavity, he thought himself an explorer, a fortune-hunter, a trailblazer so to speak, wondering what secrets he would reveal, what treasure he might find. Quickly though, things had gone downhill, in more ways than one. In the blink of an eye, a wide, gently meandering, slow moving subterranean river system had transformed without any notice into a tightly packed, fast flowing, white water nightmare, turning him head over heels, making him lose any sort of sense of direction, throwing him into rock faces, all the time taking him further and further underground. Panic had started to settle in as ups and downs became viciously violent and stomach churning, even for a being such as himself. The final indignity arrived out of nowhere as the underground waterway briefly opened up into a massive cavern on a scale he'd never seen or heard of before, and his kind had spent many centuries scouting out this part of the planet.

Unfortunately for him, he didn't have a chance to peruse it in the way he would have liked. Just as he started to take in his surroundings, the water fell away as he tumbled clumsily over the biggest waterfall he'd ever seen in his entire life, easily three hundred metres high, disappearing into a dark hole, the bottom of which was nowhere near visible. A sense of immediate self preservation kicked in and he cast what he thought of as his most powerful, all encompassing shield. Whether it would be enough, only the next few moments would tell, as he writhed and twisted, tumbled and turned, all in mid-air, all surrounded by the icy cold water that he considered his friend. Fleetingly, thoughts of the others washed over him. Terror tortured his mind at the thought of dying here, his friends and family never knowing his twisted fate. And then a fast flowing body of water hit him, knocking the wind out of him, momentarily rendering him unconscious. Dangerous beyond belief, luckily for him thinking on his feet (or tail in this case) in the form of using his ancient magic had at least temporarily saved his life. Sealed inside a magical shell, the thunderous white water propelled him on his underwater journey, bouncing him this way and that, giving him no inkling of exactly where he was, or where he was headed. Slowly he regained his wits, thankful to have survived the massive drop of the waterfall. Delving into all his magic, something only really ever done in a time of need, he figured this applied now more than at any other point in his short life. Conjuring up three brilliant blue balls of ferociously stunning light, through serpent-like eyes he scanned the enclosed underground river ahead, hoping for any kind of way out, or sign of exactly where he was. This continued for some time, with the body of water he found himself trapped in, slowing ever so slightly. Buoyed by this, he flooded his bumps and bruises with a little ethereal power, instantly washing away the pain, still maintaining the shield that had almost certainly saved his life. Free from the distraction of his wounds, and with a clear head for the first time in a while, it was then that he spotted it... a vague and mysterious white light, shining down on the right hand side of the river, directly in front of him. With a flick of his tail, he lowered his shield and glided seamlessly in that direction, hoping to find some form of salvation. If only he knew the momentous effect of what he was about to do would have on history itself. Perhaps then he'd have continued with his underwater journey.

Having been summarily dismissed by his father without injury, Man pondered what he should do. Lessons were a while off starting, and he had little desire to go and hang about the amphitheatre. He supposed that if he hurried, he could catch up with his brother at the prisoner. After all, he'd probably only just finished collecting the food by now. If he got a move on, he'd possibly arrive at exactly the same time. Decision made, he turned and, at not quite a run, headed off into the darkest depths of the icy white prison, to find the friendly face of his sibling, and the unluckiest prisoner in the whole world.

Strolling around the mammoth icy wall that separated out this part of the encampment, if that's what you could call it, he could just make out the prisoner, curled up as much as possible, in all likelihood asleep. Out of nowhere, a voice from the direction he'd just come startled him, almost causing him to drop the sack of food he was carrying.

"Josh, Josh hold on."

A small smile crept across his face at the sight of his brother jogging along towards him. Instantly his disposition turned from dark and cloudy, to sunny and hot.

"What are you doing here? I thought you'd be with Father all day. Are you alright?"

"I'm fine, I'm fine," panted Man, his frozen breath extending quite a long way out in front of him from his exertions. "I don't doubt I'll be back there again in the near future. I'm just glad I caught up with you."

"Me too."

"Shall we?" asked Man, indicating with his outstretched arm that they should head over towards the captive dragon.

Josh led the way.

Getting as close as was safely possible, Man spoke up, his words a soft breeze floating on the wind against a backdrop of running water.

"Are you awake, dragon? We've brought you some food."

Slowly, scales moved, wings rustled and eyelids rolled back. It looked to be a very taxing process today.

"I am just about awake... thank you."

"It doesn't seem fair that you get to sleep at all," growled Josh, not the biggest fan in the world of Unlucky.

"Josh!" exclaimed Man. "Enough! I know you don't like him and begrudge doing these chores, but they're the ones we've been set and it's our duty to see it out to the best of our ability. What would Mother say if she could see and hear you now? She wouldn't be best pleased, would she?"

"I suppose not."

"So suck it up. Good manners cost nothing. You don't have to like him, or the job, but there's no need to be rude and insulting. I know you're better than that."

Suitably reprimanded, Josh's face showed just how deeply sorry he was. As Man turned back to face the dragon prisoner, once again he noticed fresh, deep welts covered in a dirty layer of dried green blood. About to ask about the new injuries, suddenly the biggest 'SPLASH' in the world, interrupted them, from the direction of the underground river. All three turned to see what had happened.

From out of the ice cold running water that sat beneath the flickering electric light above it, leapt a quasi-humanoid, with a snake shaped body, and a top half resembling a scaly reptilian human. With a tail about six metres long, it rippled with muscle, scale and teeth. Gun metal grey for the most part, tiny blotches of light yellow sat scattered down the left hand side of its tail, looking as though an artist had flicked paint at it with a brush. Momentarily stunned, not one of them could break the deafening silence that sat over the four of them, against the backdrop of the stream. Crystal clear chilling cold water streamed down the naga's body (as that's what he was) mostly freezing before it hit the frosty ground.

Josh was the first to react, and not in a good way. Tossing his sack at the dragon prisoner, he spun around and at great speed, headed back the way he'd come, all the time at the top of his voice, screaming,

"Oh my God, oh my God!"

The two remaining occupants of this awful environment remained calm, both in their own ways excited about this new arrival. Deep within the dragon prisoner's mind, thoughts of escape and freedom ran riot, hoping against hope that this might be his chance.

For Man it was slightly different. Never having been taught about the varying array of creatures that existed on this planet, the being before him seemed completely alien and different to anything he could ever have imagined. But being the kind, peaceful and good spirited individual he was, there was never going to be anything but a warm and generous welcome.

"Uhhhhh... hi," was all that he could manage to utter.

Having slipped on the ice on landing, the naga had remained for the most part on the floor, with only its head raised. As Man stood there waiting for a response, it grew to its full height, its upper half weaving from side to side like a deadly, venomous cobra.

Dumbstruck at finding humans and dragons here, of all places, one of the harshest environments on the planet, the serpent-like beast threw all its magic at the two of them in an effort to better understand the situation.

A purple/pink haze sparkled into life around both Man and the dragon prisoner, bubbling, hissing and spitting as it did so. Remaining calm, the prisoner knew exactly what was going on, because he'd heard about it some time ago in a lecture. The naga was using his magic to see exactly who he was dealing with and just what language was being used. He'd heard that they could use their abilities to translate their tongue into any known tongue.

Rising fear started to overtake Man, causing doubts about his course of action. Perhaps the wise thing would have been to run and get help like his brother had. Reinforcements would be a welcome relief about now. But as quickly as it had come, the ethereal power unleashed by the naga fizzled out totally.

Waiting to see what happened next, both the dragon prisoner and Man were stunned when the naga spoke up.

"Good morrow, I bid you greetings. It's nice to meet you and I apologise profoundly if I've offended you by stumbling onto your territory by accident."

"It's not a problem," observed Man. "It was just such a shock seeing you. I've never seen your kind before. Can I ask what you are, if it's not too rude?"

Smiling, which was more than a little odd on a being looking like that, the sea monster replied.

"I'm a naga, and like the rest of my race I'm suited to the cold and can survive both in and out of the water."

"Wow!" exclaimed Man.

"Wow indeed," said the naga. "I have to say, I didn't expect to find..."

He nearly said humans, but his magic had stumbled across the truth as it had examined both beings.

"...dragons here, so far underground, so far out of their comfort zone."

"It's a long story," announced Man, shivering in the cold.

The naga's ethereal power had also discovered something else... a hint of potential, buried, hiding away through no fault of its own, restless and scared, afraid that it would never see the light of day. The naga knew he could help with that, and so in the spirit of friendship, and with the tiny fingers on both of his hands whirring away, he cast one of the ancient spells that he'd been taught long ago, and let his magic, enhance that of his newfound friend.

Pain, at least that's what he'd thought had overcome him, deep inside.

'An attack,' he thought, frightened for his life. A split second later, it became obvious that was not the case, as a familiar feeling expanded out from his stomach, flooding his limbs and head. Drowning in ecstasy, that's how it felt as the magic within him was ignited into action. Eyes closed, head pointed upwards, he felt both as light as a feather and heavier than lead. A sensation of expansion tickled every part of him as every emotion under the sun battered his physical form. Tattered rags whipped around the air in front of him. Briefly he wondered where they'd come from, but with his mind trying to cope with a myriad of thoughts, that particular one was soon dismissed. Perfection personified was how it felt as every atom in his body burned with the magical energy unlocked. It was the greatest moment of his life.

Unlucky looked on in fascination, wondering what on earth was happening. He'd long since suspected that there was something different about these younger captives who were pledged to look after him, but he hadn't known what. If he'd thought it through, he might just about have put the pieces of the puzzle together. But with the constant battering of the cold, lack of magic due to the temperatures, constant hunger and the desperation bombarding him all the time, his thinking was nothing like it should be. But now, he was about to find out the truly terrifying truth. It was far from the greatest moment of his life.

"HELP... HELP... HELP!" screamed Josh at the top of his voice, his words booming around the cavern as he ran.

Those going about their daily routines watched in fascination as the youth sprinted along the path towards their leader's quarters. Puffing heavily, scared out of his mind and worried beyond belief for his brother's safety, he slid to a halt on the outer reach of his father's accommodation, still screaming his head off. Two of the guards approached, wary of what was going on, knowing exactly who he was, and just how much their leader despised him.

"HELP, HELP... you must help! A monstrous creature's thrown itself out of the underground stream near the dragon prisoner. My brother's there, all on his own, defenceless."

"WHAT THE HELL IS ALL THIS COMOTION?" bellowed the leader, storming around the corner and out into the confusion.

Panting furiously, the usual fear gripped Josh at the sight of his father heading his way.

"SPIT IT OUT BOY!" yelled his father, absolutely livid, the veins in his neck pumping two to the dozen, his face taking on a dark purple hue.

Concern for his brother was all that got Josh through the next few seconds.

"A monstrous creature's thrown itself out of the underground stream near the dragon prisoner. Man's there all defenceless and alone. You have to help, you have to help!"

Josh's father stood there for a moment, quietly contemplating what his runt of a son had told him. One thought, and one thought alone playing through his mind: this was it. The stroke of luck that they needed... it had been a long time in the coming, but if they used their initiative, then just maybe they would get out of this hellhole after all.

Without hesitation, he ordered all his guards to follow him, before turning and sprinting off in the direction of the trouble, his men following in his wake.

Back by the stream, magic had taken hold. For a split second Man had passed out, or at least that's how it appeared. For the life of him, he couldn't remember the last few seconds, although the stinging rapture from just before that was ingrained in his very DNA, something never to be forgotten. Filled with elation, Man started to pick himself up off the floor. Abruptly, he felt weary and tired, almost as though he'd been drained of energy. Leaning his head over his shoulder, it was then that he spotted it. On the floor directly behind him, was what looked like a huge ice blue crystalline mace.

'How odd,' he thought, as his gaze followed the length of the bizarre object. Arcing round slowly, the crystalline structure then began to merge with beautifully constructed turquoise scales that expanded in size, the further he moved along the appendage. Mind all of a fluster, he felt as though he were having the ultimate out of body experience.

'It can't be true... it just can't,' he thought, as the extent of what he could see behind him was stopped by just how far his neck could crane.

Only then did it occur to him to look straight down in front of him. On doing so, he nearly peed his pants, or at least he would have done, had the remnants of them not fluttered off to the four corners of the cavern he stood in.

'Oh crap!' was the next thought to form in his wildly spinning brain.

Huge, blue scaled legs with muscle and sinew bulging at the seams stood out from the brilliant white of his surroundings. Glistening, light blue and white crystal stalactites jutted out from every part of the prehistoric body he found himself looking at. Instinctively he stood up, astounded as the gigantic, scaly legs did so in unison with his command. Standing up tall, a new sensation prickled his brain as powerful wings unfolded to their true extent. Turning a full one hundred and eighty degrees, he stared disbelievingly into the reflective icy sheen of the wall, agog at what stood before him. A dragon, and not just any dragon, but an almighty one at that. Several shades of blue, needle sharp crystalline spines poked out from nearly every part of his body. White, perfectly formed eyes stared back at him, his head and jaw surrounded by these strange spikes. It was both terrifying and electric at the same time.

A short way away, Unlucky, the dragon prisoner, looked on, both amazed and terrified, because his mind had just pieced together everything playing out around him.

'They've procreated naturally, and hoped their magic will get transferred and built up that way. If that's what they've done, then there's a huge threat about to be released. I've got to break free and warn them, I just have to.'

Invigorated by everything going on, once more he rallied against the cold and the chains that bound him in place. Not for the first time, this had little or no effect. All he could do was watch history unfold.

"What have you done?" roared Man, rolling his long neck from side to side.

"Just jump-started the magic within you. It was always there ready to go, it just needed a little nudge to come out and play. I hope you don't mind, it seemed like the right thing to do."

"Mind?" put in Man, "It's the best thing that's ever happened to me. I can't thank you enough."

At that exact moment, the community's leader came flying around the corner into the cavern, followed hot on his heels by six burly looking guards.

Man's father and his guards did an emergency stop, slamming on the brakes, all of them nearly toppling like dominoes.

"What in the name of...?"

A huge, blue, prehistoric head turned to face the newcomers. Inside, Man liked how it felt to see the fear on not only the guard's faces, but his father's as well. Who was in control now?!

Pushing his momentary bout of shock aside, Man's father gathered up his thoughts and strode purposefully into the fray, just like the leader that he was. Approaching the naga, and ignoring the gargantuan beast off to one side that he now knew was his favoured son, he respectfully bowed his head towards the still dripping wet, serpent-like monster and with his best diplomatic face, offered up all the wisdom and sincerity that he had.

"It's a privilege to meet you. I am the leader of this collective. We would be honoured if you would stay a while as our guest."

Sensing nothing but truth and honesty from the shape in front of him, the naga bowed his huge snake-like head, returning the leader's simple gesture.

"I would be delighted to stay as your guest. It's a pleasure to meet you. My given name is Margett, but you're welcome to call me Marg."

"Well met Marg," ventured Man's father. "Can I ask, what have you done to this one?"

"On arriving, I sensed a great deal of conflict deep beneath the surface of his psyche, a squabbling of sorts. On closer inspection, it would appear the magic contained within was trying to break free. All I did was provide it with a conduit to do so. After that, nature took its course, transforming him into what you see before you."

"Impressive," stated their leader. "Can you do that for all of us?"

"Until I meet the individuals concerned, it would be impossible to tell I'm afraid."

"What about me?" he asked hungrily.

Closing his dark grey eyelids, Marg stood tall, his upper body swaying like an oak tree in the wind, his lower body and tail keeping him firmly rooted to the ground.

After half a minute or so, the naga opened his eyes and spoke.

"I can find nothing within you. Not a drop of supernatural power or an inkling of magic. I would surmise that constant exposure to the cold has contained the spark you speak of, so much so, that it's currently impossible to find."

Inside, the leader raged. Outwardly, there was no sign of it.

"Well thank you for taking a look. It means a lot."

The lies floated off his lips like butterflies in the wind.

"If you would allow it, I'll send my men to get word to the others in an effort to prepare something special. For as long as we've been here, we've never had a visitor. You're quite the rarity and everyone will be deeply pleased to see you."

"That sounds dandy."

"All of you," stated the leader, "go back to the others and get them to prepare a feast of epic proportions."

"Yes sir," they all said simultaneously, before darting off round the corner.

Out of the corner of one eye, the leader could just see the abject terror on the dragon prisoner's face.

'Ahhh...' he thought, 'he must have only just put together what's happened. Good for him, good for him.'

Turning to face his son, a quick inspection had him deeply impressed, especially with the crystalline spikes jutting out at all angles. A formidable beast indeed, and able to withstand the cold in that form.

'What great potential resides within you,' he thought.

"Impressive... Man. You must be over the moon."

"I feel honoured to be able to touch my magic so. This form feels like it's always been part of me."

"To a greater or lesser degree, it always has," replied his father, knowing full well there was a very good chance that magic unlike anything ever seen on this planet now resided deep inside his son. For the very first time it occurred to him that he had to be careful. Nurturing the ethereal power within the boy might be the only way to escape. Offering out an olive branch might be the way to go. It went against every instinct he had. Now was not the time though, to let personal feelings get in the way.

Strolling up to the mighty blue and white prehistoric form his son found himself in, the leader patted one of his giant scaled legs in admiration, a tiny smirk forming across his face.

"You know I'm proud of you... son? Your efforts will lead all of us out of this place one day, of that I'm certain. And then you can take your rightful place in the order of things, and once more we'll be able to shape the planet back to how it should be. Have faith, practise those abilities, nurture your magic, and help your peers to do the same. You're an inspiration to everyone here. Don't forget that."

Those words, creating that feeling, would be something Man would remember for the rest of his life. Never had he heard his father talk that way to anyone, least of all him. The magic within him, it would seem, had changed everything. Now he could bring everyone here together, in one common goal, and maybe with the naga's help they could once and for all leave this place. Like all the others, he'd heard stories about the outside world, but never thought until today that he might at some point have a chance to see it for himself. As fantastical as it had sounded, when some of the others had talked about it, now it almost seemed within touching distance. What a life, he, Josh and his mother could have if they all escaped this place. Today was the start of that journey towards their new existence.

With a solid purpose in mind, their leader, Man's father, escorted their naga guest away from the dragon prisoner, but not before asking his son to return to his human guise. As the disappointment registered on his face, Man was buoyed by his father's encouragement, telling him he should practise switching between the two forms at least twice a day, and discover all the abilities his prehistoric persona presented itself with. Nodding eagerly, he watched his father and the naga slip effortlessly around the corner and out of sight, leaving him alone in the cavern with Unlucky, the dragon prisoner, the sound of running water piercing the freezing air.

"An impressive creation, youngster," observed Unlucky from across the way.

"Thank you," boomed Man's ancient and guttural voice back in his direction.

"You know you're different to all the others, don't you?" asked Unlucky.

"I'm just like everyone else... I have a mother and father, all the right bits in all the right places."

Head spinning faster than a circular saw blade cutting concrete, Unlucky could barely get his mind around everything that was going on. Often he'd wondered how these youngsters had appeared here, in this place. Not once had he ever come close to the right answer, despite devoting weeks at a time to thinking about it. But that wasn't the biggest surprise. Discovering Man, one of the two young men to come and feed him on a regular basis, not only had magical power, but could take the form of a dragon, was absolutely astounding. Not once in all the time they'd been bringing him food, had he ever got even an inkling that such a thing existed. And he should have sensed something, no matter how small, at some point. None of it made any sense. That is, until you cast away the improbable, and looked at what you're left with, which terrified the absolute life out of him, given everything that had gone on over the last half an hour or so.

"Your magic," continued Unlucky, "it's different, dark dangerous magic, because of how you were conceived."

"I don't understand," remarked Man, thinking about

trying to revert back to his human form.

"The others... they're all dragons, stuck in their human form. You... you're a human that can take dragon form. Very different, almost dangerously so. You need to be careful Man... watch not only your magic, but your back as well. Potentially you're more powerful than anyone else here, maybe anywhere on the planet. Use what you have wisely, and let that intrigue, wonder and kind heart that you have, win through and I'm sure everything will be as it should."

"Thank you... I think."

And with that, Man managed to unlock the bonds of the beast that he'd become and in but an instant reverted back to his ape-like form. Unfortunately for him, he'd forgotten that the tattered rags he'd come to regard as his clothes had dispersed into the wind, no good to anyone now. And so, naked and cold, covering his tiny modesty with both hands, he staggered off around the corner, shivering intently, wondering where he'd find something else to wear, forgetting all about the fresh wounds to the dragon prisoner he was responsible for.

Not a natural diplomat by any means, the community leader had sucked up his discomfort and had made their naga visitor feel as at home as possible, on a short tour of their underground encampment, showing him how they grew their food, the amphitheatre where the youngsters were taught, the electric lighting systems sustained by rigidly imposed mantras and the male sleeping quarters, all of which the naga appeared to be impressed by. Nothing was said about the impoverished state of those all around, the lack of hope apparent, or the squalor and poverty that they all resided in. Man's father let it linger in the air, a question unasked for the time being at least, hoping that the naga's quick thinking brain would at some point bring it up of his own accord. Of course it would be better that way, and would play right into his hands.

Excusing himself in favour of one of his men continuing the tour, he feigned having to oversee preparations for the planned meal. Their guest bought it, hook, line and sinker.

Returning to his quarters, the leader was glad to see Man waiting there for him, having been fetched by two of his guards. Off in one corner, a makeshift pile of scrap wood had been cobbled together. Something unusual was going on.

With little time to spare, he turned to his son and nodded in the direction of the scrap pile of wood.

"Light it!" he ordered, his voice clear that it was a command.

"I...I...I...I..."

"Light it now! I don't care whether you use your magic in your current form, or change back into that prehistoric monster and light it with your breath. There's no time for games. Get it done... NOW!"

Terrified to his very core at the menace behind his father's words, Man reached within himself for the spark that had been transformed into a raging fire by the lost and befriended naga. Immediately he found it, and so reaching out with his right hand towards the damp, dank wood, he urged the power inside him to flow steadily out. Not quite in the way he would have wished, a stuttering stream of flame erupted from his fingers, singeing the scrap pieces at first, before eventually setting them alight.

A tension of epic proportions building between them, the leader stomped on over to his son. For Man's part, he quite literally had no idea what would happen next. Would psycho Father poke his head, or more likely his fist out, and make an appearance, or would the more shy, reserved and polite personality give it a go? Who knew? Not him, not even after all this time, that was for sure. Nervous as hell, he waited to see just what his raffle prize would be.

"I'm sorry I shouted," announced his father, sounding

completely and utterly genuine.

His son, however, had heard it all before, and failed to fall for it.

"It's just that there's so much going on, the arrival of our new guest, some of the food's been tainted recently, running our stocks precariously low. The pressure's really started to tell, more so now than at any time I can remember."

With very little space between the two of them now, as Man gazed into his father's eyes there did seem to be an authentic plea there, something resembling honesty at least, compelling an almost automatic reaction from the young boy dragon.

"I'm sorry Father. I know you're under a lot of stress most of the time. If there's ever anything I can do to help, you know that you only have to ask."

Glassy eyed, his father started to well up, something that shocked Man to his very core, having never once having seen this happen.

"That's very nice of you to say that son, and who knows, maybe one day I'll take you up on that. But for now, I'll probably only need you to apply your considerable will to the magic. That in itself will be a great help, and may well move us one step closer to leaving this despicable place, once and for all. Do you think you can do that?"

"Sure thing... whatever you need."

"That's my boy," declared the leader proudly, moving closer and in an even bigger shock, hugging his offspring, something that had definitely never happened before.

Man relished every moment.

At exactly the same time, his father, deep within his mind, unleashed something he'd been saving up since before he'd been incarcerated here. One word.

'SURRIPERE!' which in an ancient tongue somewhere, meant STEAL!

It was in essence very much a magical one off shot, a

last chance at jump-starting his magic. If the word was pronounced with all of a being's willpower behind it, (as it had been) and there was magic in the immediate vicinity, supposedly it would pilfer just a tiny amount of power, siphoning it off without the other being knowing it. The leader had high hopes for this, and had secreted it away in the back of his mind for a very long time. He'd almost used it in that very last fight all that time ago, but with all the chaos that ensued, the chance hadn't presented itself. As well, you see, it was a onetime thing. For whatever unexplained supernatural reason, a being could only use this particular mantra once in their lifetime. After that, it would never work, which was no doubt due to some magical side effect. While Man's father didn't think for a moment that it would kick start his magical birthright, he had what can only be described as a cunning plan to use that tiny spark, in an effort to gain a roaring flame, something that could well save them all. For decades he'd sought out the tiniest inkling of magic, in the hope of using this mantra, but of course there was nothing here in this vile place. Not one of the beings trapped here had possessed even the tiniest amount of accessible magic, and that included the traitorous prisoner that his sons had the displeasure to feed every day. That's right, he'd even scouted him out as potential... but still NOTHING!

When he'd first clapped eyes on the naga, that had all changed. But it would have been too much of a risk to try it out on him. If something in his alien physiology caused a problem, then it was all for nothing. But his son... wow, what an opportunity! And of course the magic should work just fine. After all, he was still a dragon, albeit not one created in quite the same way. The thoughts of freedom and revenge tugging away at his insides disappeared instantly, he enabling him to shrug off fantasy and return to reality with a bump.

Pulling away as quickly as he'd stepped in, aware of the stunned expression of his son, he nodded his head in recognition of what had just happened, pleased that once again he'd managed to totally and utterly hoodwink the boy. Gullibility like that was rare to find, he thought. Back to their pre-perceived roles, things continued as they should have.

"Good," announced his father. "You may go for now. Rest assured though, your talents will be in great demand over the next few days."

Eager to leave, and not having to be told twice, Man marched out of the doorway and, once out of sight of his father's men, sprinted for all he was worth back to the tiny space that was his.

Using makeshift metal poles from some of the massive light fittings that had been left behind for them by their captors, a rudimentary spit was created over the roaring fire in no time at all. After that, it was just a matter of fetching the meat that had been in the freezer, so to speak, for quite some time. Since they'd been imprisoned here, nothing but fruit and vegetables had been consumed by any of them. Today would be the first time for any among them to consume a dragon's favourite delicacy... roasted flesh. But the roasted flesh of what? Probably better not to know. After all, up until now, they'd never had the means to cook anything, fire was for all intents and purposes a thing of the past. With proceedings progressing at quite a pace, all everyone involved in the plan could do was cross their fingers and hope against hope that they could make their own luck and give fate the tiniest of nudges in their direction.

A short while later, their honoured guest, and only link to the outside world, adjourned to the leader's room that had been laid out appropriately, smelled heavily of roasted meat, and showed off the finest selection of food available to their humble community. Many had worked hard to put on such an occasion, with most foregoing their nightly meal. Would it all be worth it? Only time would tell.

Meanwhile, many, many thousands of miles away, in a much warmer environment, tiny little fractures started to occur across the gently curved, matt white surface of the only remaining egg left in the hatchery section of the Purbeck Peninsula nursery ring. In one darkened corner of the room, a short, round dragonling, only a few months old, with big floppy ears more suited to a rabbit, who was predominantly brown with some striking green scales thrown in for good measure in a currently unfathomable shape, sat on his arse, puffing out rings of smoke, or at least trying to, unaware of what was playing out around him.

Coughing abruptly from having inhaled when he should have exhaled, the inquisitive and slightly timid dragon failed to hear the 'CRACK' of a long, zigzagging line appearing on the solitary egg left in the room. So it came as something of a shock to him when the domed top of the egg slid off to one side and crashed unceremoniously to the floor. Jumping higher than he ever thought possible, he slunk back into the shadows of the corner he currently occupied, afraid and feeling all alone.

Through a shower of steam escaping from the top of the egg, a sparkling, emerald green, perfectly formed dragonling head poked out over the top, darting this way and that, taking in everything there was to take in.

Spine pressed firmly into both walls, as far back as he could go, the smoke blower wondered if he should run off to find one of the 'tors' and tell them what had happened. But he was too mesmerised to move, intrigued to see what would happen next.

Sniffing the air for a few precious moments, the stunning green, tiny, prehistoric head ducked out of sight briefly.

The young dragonling in the corner of the room wondered what had happened. Maybe the newcomer had exhausted all of his energy, he contemplated. Before that thought had even finished forming, a sleek, dragon form tumbled up, out and over the side of the egg, landing perfectly on two feet.

'Wow!' he thought, looking on from the shadows. 'That was amazing. Whoever he is, I'd really like to get to know him.'

Pulling in what was a huge breath from brand new yet ancient, prehistoric lungs, the new arrival rolled their head this way and that, still sniffing the air, wondering exactly where they were. It was only then that they discovered they were not alone.

A little known fact about dragons is that their inherent, ancient, magical powers exist the moment they are conceived and develop alongside them while they grow in their eggs, taking in everything around them, processing sounds, smells and movements. While the eggs are in the care of a nursery ring, it is usual for music and languages of all kinds to be played constantly, so that the maturing dragonlings have a rudimentary understanding of communication when they come into this world. Most dragons when they hatch would have the equivalent understanding of a human eight year old. This new one here seemed much more switched on than that.

"Hello," she positively purred.

Yes... SHE! That was something of a surprise to the floppy eared smoke blower, who now had little choice but to step forward, out of the darkness.

"Hi," he squeaked back.

"Are you new here too?" she asked inquisitively.

Trying to pull himself up straight, acutely aware that his form looked more than a little unconventional, he tried to deepen his voice in an effort to impress. Needless to say it didn't work.

"Uhhh... I've been here a little while... a few months I think."

"What are you doing in here?"

"Oh... we're on a break from studies. I just wanted some quiet time away from the others. They always seem to want to pick on me. I don't really know why."

"That sounds terrible."

"It just is what it is I suppose. I've not known anything else."

"Don't the grownups stop it from happening?"

"They seem to think it's better to stay out of things and let us handle our own disputes. That was something they taught us almost straight away."

"It doesn't sound right if you ask me."

"I concur one hundred percent," he agreed, his big floppy ears pricking up.

"What say you and I become friends?" asked the emerald green female, stalking ever closer, a soft shade of yellow now noticeable across her stomach.

He didn't have to think about it, not even for a split second.

"That sounds great!" he exclaimed.

"Nice to meet you," she proffered.

"Nice to meet you too," he replied.

And with that, the two friends wandered off to find the 'tors', a new friendship forged, one that would stand the test of time and maybe, at some point, even save the planet itself. If history could have taken a selfie, right at that very moment, it would have.

As the leader and his naga guest tucked into everything the icy prison had to offer, an awkward silence developed, much to his satisfaction. If the roles were reversed, he knew he'd barely be able to contain his desire to ask certain questions. He only hoped the alien looking beast's mind worked in much the same way. Moments later, he had his answer.

"I must say you cope with your situation with as much good grace as is possible. Do you mind if I ask you how you come to be out here, under all of this, in these quite devastating temperatures?"

Pausing for effect, letting as much sadness as he could muster trample all over his face, the leader, jumping up and down inside, let out a slow, deliberate, very resigned breath.

"It all happened quite some time ago."

The naga looked on in rapt attention.

"We formed an outlying part of the dragon domain, a small, secluded community that kept itself to itself. Often representatives of the dragon monarch would come by, insisting that we comply with this or that order or law, trying to bind us to their will in one way or another. We would of course respect their views, whilst trying to present our own. Eventually we were granted a representative on their council. It was a way of life for us that lasted over a century without much complaint or argument."

Man's father "tried" unsuccessfully to stifle the tears that were building behind his eyes. The naga was moved, hooked on every word. As the tears flowed, and the laughter inside was pushed away, the leader resumed where he'd left off.

Suddenly, out of the blue one day, a delegation of dragons and five squads of guards arrived without warning. It was a shock to all of us. But that was nothing to what followed. We were threatened with eviction from the land that belonged to us, and had to our fathers, and our fathers' fathers before that. A scuffle ensued, but we were badly outmatched and for the sake of the dragonlings amongst us, we stood down, cowed before those who would do us harm. On hearing of our predicament, our councillor brought the case in front of the council, all to no avail. For a brief period, we were prisoners in our own homes, our resources plundered by those we stood side by side with. None of us knew what was going on. Undeterred, our representative in the capital plugged away at the bureaucracy, trying to find out exactly what had happened. It turned out that a diabolical, underhanded plot to take control of the planet had been underway for many, many decades. Our councillor stumbled onto it quite by accident and managed to find the resistance that had been rallying against it for quite some time. It cost the councillor his life, but he managed to get word back to us about exactly what was going on. In his last missive, he mentioned that the dragon king himself had sent out orders that the world's ancient races were to be hunted down to extinction. That was enough to convince all of us to join the rebellion against such demented evil. At the last minute though, we were tricked and captured, held against our will, our homes and lands pillaged and ruined."

The naga's eyes remained wide with shock, so outrageous was the story. But not at any point did he doubt anything that he'd heard.

Taking a small sip of water before carrying on, the cunning leader delved deeper into his wicked box of dark lies.

"Rounded up as a community and held deep underground, starving and afraid, it looked for all intents and purposes as though we'd be killed as an example to anyone else that fought against their cause. But that was not to be, because they had a much crueller punishment in mind, something we could never have imagined."

Man's father paused, swallowing awkwardly, visibly upset, barely able to continue.

The naga, completely gullible, having swallowed every last word, filled in the gap.

"They brought you here... didn't they?"

Man's father could only nod in confirmation.

"How long ago was this?" asked the serpent-like beast.

Having long since planned all this, the words floated

convincingly off the leader's lips.

"Over one hundred years ago now, although being stuck here makes it impossible to tell exactly."

This time it was the naga's turn to nod in understanding.

"And you've survived here like this during all of that time?"

"Yes....it's been a struggle, and I've tried to lead as best I can, but honestly... I don't know how we've coped. At times, it's been one tragedy after another. Cave-ins, accidents, you name it, it's happened, pretty much all of which would have been preventable with our magic. But as you've seen, the cold has held it in check, making us nothing more than onlookers during these desperate times."

It was a true tale of woe, or at least that's how the ancient, reptilian beast viewed it.

Taking stock, the two sat there in silence for quite a few minutes, until at last the naga broke it.

"Over the course of the last two decades, I've never heard of our kind coming into conflict with dragons."

"I don't suppose you would," uttered the leader dejectedly. "From what little I can remember, you as a race, because of where you reside, were very much last on their list. For dragons to come for you, would take almost all of their magic to stave off the cold. It would be a Herculean task, one that they'd have to devote all their resources to. I would imagine they'd get rid of the others first, before going after you."

The naga seriously contemplated the words. It was only then that the leader tried to close the deal.

"Have you heard from any of the other ancient races?"

It was a gambit of course, but a very calculated one at that. Over the course of time, each of the races had drifted apart, finding their own little niche on planet earth, determined to stay off the radar, letting the humans make their own way, well, all apart from the dragon domain that is. The leader was counting on exactly this, right here, right now.

"As far as I know, there's been no contact with any of the other races for a very long time. Of course I'm not privileged to any information our king might have."

"I see."

Once again silence encompassed them, as the frost hung in the air, both beings' breath freezing as they exhaled, much to the pleasure of one, and the disappointment of the other.

"From everything that you've told me, it seems clear that I need to get word to our king urgently. If the other races have been taken out of the picture then it would be up to us to fight back. Any and all information you could provide would be very welcome indeed, I'm sure."

"Of course, it would be our pleasure to share," stated the leader, knowingly.

"Do you think you would be able to help us escape this intolerable prison? It's not so much for me that I ask, more for all of those under my guidance. The toll it's taken on them is great, and it breaks my heart every time I walk around our meagre encampment."

"I don't see why not," ventured Marg. "As a race we control much coveted, ancient magic that has the potential to do almost anything. Of course, it's not my decision to make, and only the king will be able to choose. But since you've already provided such vital information, and have agreed to help us out going forward, I can't see anything getting in the way."

Inside, the leader's cold, black heart, jumped for joy. They were so close he could almost touch the outside world. One or two more things had to go their way, but he couldn't foresee anything going wrong from now on. All he had to do was to continue to act the part, and that he was sure he could do.

"Can I ask about the boy, the one whose magic I set free?"

"Of course," declared Man's father, eager to hear his visitor's thoughts on the subject. It should, if nothing else, offer up a very unique perspective, he thought.

"How is it his magic is different to yours, and that I can sense and enhance his, but not anyone else's here?"

A lie combined with a healthy dose of the truth seemed to be the best course of action. It was all too slick in coming out.

"Marooned here with very little in the way of resources, for a very long time, all we did was try and find a way out. After a couple of decades, it became obvious that without our magic, we were doomed to fail. And so most of those here gave up, and became resigned to their fate. All thoughts of escape gone by the wayside, relationships formed, and with our bodies transformed so accurately into our human personas, after a short while, the inevitable happened. Women folk began to fall pregnant, and one by one children were born. No thought was given to magic; after all, we truly believed it to be totally dormant within us all, and had absolutely no idea that it could, or would, be passed on. In fact, it only became apparent a couple of years ago, that one or two youthful individuals may in fact be harbouring some kind of unique magical energy. Up until you enhanced my son's power earlier today, we'd never seen any kind of results to show that it physically existed."

"I'm sorry... I didn't know that he was your son. I hope I haven't offended you by augmenting his power."

"Not at all, not at all. What you did was just confirm our suspicions, and give him a chance to access his birthright. I couldn't be happier."

That last sentence was totally, and utterly the truth, but probably not in the way the naga saw it.

"I'm glad that you see it that way."

"So am I, so am I. Can I ask just how you think we should proceed from here on in?"

A studious expression gripping his face, the naga

thought long and hard for a few moments, before finally replying.

"I think I need to contact my king, and let him know about the threat we face from the dragons. I could try and reach out telepathically from in here, but I'm pretty sure I'm too far away from any of my race for it to be successful."

"It's worth a try though, don't you think?" added Man's father, believing that this would be the perfect outcome. Getting the naga king here without losing their leverage in the form of Marg would be the ideal scenario as far as he was concerned.

"If you could find me some total and utter solitude, then I would gladly give it a go. It might take more than a few hours to even try. If successful though, it would save us a whole lot of time."

"If it worked, what would likely happen?"

"In theory if I could find one of my kind, they might be able to amplify the message and forward it straight on to the king. Given everything I now know, I would assume the monarch would want to come directly here, as soon as possible."

Boy did that sound good.

"And you'd be able to give him directions to get here?"

"I'm pretty sure I could remember enough to get him close. After that, he and his team would have no problem homing in on me so to speak. I'd imagine he'd want to hear the details of your story first hand, but I find it hard to believe that he wouldn't want to help you and everyone here."

"That sounds terrific," replied the leader, already piecing the final parts of the puzzle together in his head. "How soon can we get started?"

"How soon can you find me the solitude that I need to focus my mind?"

"If you come right this way, I'll show you straight there myself."

And with that, the two of them left the humble, ice cold room, both of them with very different ideas as to what would happen next.

Lessons over for the day, Josh and Man hooked up and headed off in the direction of their mother, having already agreed to join her for a meal.

Having not spoken a word to each other throughout the day, Josh was keen to ask Man what had happened back at the dragon prisoner's cave.

"What on earth happened and why the hell didn't you get out of there when you had the chance?" queried the younger of the two brothers.

Having played out the events over and over in his mind during the course of the day, Man wondered just how much he should tell his brother. If he told him everything, he would worry beyond belief. But they were brothers, and secrets were hard to keep between the two of them.

"He belongs to a race called the nagas, and had gotten lost, hence the reason he threw himself up and out of the stream."

"That's incredible," declared Josh, gobsmacked.

"And that's not even the best part."

"Really?"

"Apparently his race possesses rare and ancient magic. In an instant, he was able to sense my gift locked away inside me and set it free. It was absolutely awesome."

"Wow," was all that Josh could utter.

Man continued on.

"Here's where it gets interesting. Whatever he did to me unlocked the bonds of the DNA inside me. From the moment his power touched me, I started to change."

"What did it feel like?"

"Bliss! An overwhelming infusion of scarily hot magic washing over me, charging and changing my atoms in almost a domino effect. Before I knew it, I'd transformed into what we've always been told was inside us, and what was supposedly never possible in this particular environment."

"A... dragon?"

"Yep! And not just any one at that."

"Could you see what you looked like?"

"Through the reflection on some of the walls I caught a glimpse."

"And?"

"A scaly, prehistoric body, the likes of which I could never even dream, had consumed my consciousness. Several shades of blue encompassed the whole thing, with piercing white crystalline structures jutting out at odd and jaunty angles from just about everywhere... my wings, tail, upper body. It was momentous and the most amazing experience of my life."

"What happened after that?" Josh questioned.

"Father turned up with some of his men."

Josh's eyes looked as though they were about to explode.

"And?"

"I'm not really sure. He took one look at me, told he how proud he was and then after exchanging a few words with the naga, they left together. He told me I had to practise shifting in and out of my dragon form, and that the time was nearly upon us. I'm not sure what it all means."

Josh let out a long, slow breath, the molecules in the air freezing as he did so. Bursting with excitement, he just had to ask.

"Please can I see you in your dragon form?"

"Really? Here, now?"

"Please."

Looking around to make sure there was no one about, not wanting to get caught out in the open like this, Man gave in to his brother's wishes, and started to think about the primordial power that lay deep within him. Before that first thought had even begun to flourish, common sense took over.

Without shame or hesitation, he started to strip off in the deserted, ice cold part of the cavern they found themselves in.

"What the hell are you doing?" asked his brother.

Pulling off the last of his newly gained rags, and throwing them to one side, he calmly answered.

"I've already lost one set of clothes today, and I don't intend on losing another."

Josh could only look on in disbelief.

Naked and frozen, the youngster delved deep inside and found the brilliant flame that now burnt bright. Almost as if flicking a switch, the magic inside him began to cascade out of control, like a river bursting its banks.

As Josh stood wide-eyed and open-mouthed, Man's ape-like form sparkled and sizzled, hissed and shimmered, eventually blurring out entirely, all in the blink of an eye. Before he knew it, his brother's appearance had grown considerably in stature, all of it though still very hazy and almost impossible to focus in on.

With little fuss, and about two seconds after it had started, a gigantic, monstrous prehistoric visage appeared in Man's place, rolling its mighty head from side to side, looking like something out of most people's nightmares.

More than a little afraid, Josh started to back off slightly, wondering what would come next.

Opening his stunning blue wings, taking two pounding steps forward, Man lowered his body and brought his massive scaled head to within a few inches of his sibling's terrified face.

"BOO!"

"Aaaarrrrrgggghhhhh!" screamed Josh, slipping and falling flat on his arse.

"Ha ha ha. Don't be afraid, brother," rumbled a low, guttural voice.

Slowly, Josh sat up, unable to take his eyes off his

brother's reincarnation.

"I told you it was good, didn't I?"

Josh nodded his agreement. It was the most fantastical thing he'd ever seen, even outstripping his dreams by a considerable margin.

"You look awesome," was all that he could think to say.

"Thank you."

"How does it feel?"

"It just feels right... like it was meant to be."

"Have you tried flying yet?"

That surprised Man, mainly because it hadn't even crossed his mind.

"No... I haven't really thought about it."

"How cool would that be though?" Josh ventured.

"It would be cool," admitted Man, his massive, ancient head turning to the ceiling, wondering if there were enough space to make an attempt here and now.

"I don't think there's room at the moment."

Josh nodded in agreement.

"What about breathing fire? Have you tried that?" asked the younger of the two.

This was something Man hadn't even thought about experimenting with again, so preoccupied had he become with everything else going on around him.

"SHALL I TRY IT?" boomed an inquisitive prehistoric voice.

"Ooooh... go on then."

Drawing in a huge breath, the scales on his beautiful, blue belly rippling ever so slightly as he did so, Man closed his eyes and searched inside himself for something... hot!

Patience running out, Josh willed his brother on, desperate to see even the tiniest sliver of flame. Careful what you wish for.

Abruptly, he found it. The only way to describe it was an extension of his magic, something that fought to break free. With just a thought, Man set it on its way, and then began to exhale.

Opening his eyes, hopeful of seeing some sort of reaction as the air travelled up his lungs and out of his mouth, disappointment started to set in as nothing visible emerged.

Hanging on tenterhooks, Josh's palpable excitement died away as his brother continued to breathe out.

With over half the breath gone, out of nowhere scorching, magical heat ignited in Man's throat. Caught in a mixture of confusion and surprise, immediately he tried to close his mouth. That just made things worse. Starting to choke in an effort to contain that which wanted to escape, a few brief coughs and snorts later, the older brother, magnificent in all his prehistoric glory, thrust his lethal looking jaws open wide, and closed his eyes in relief.

Josh, about to ask his brother what on earth was going on, managed to use his cat-like reactions to dive full throttle out of the way at the exact moment his brother opened his mouth, narrowly missing the streaking ball of red, orange, yellow and blue flaming fire. With a huge 'BOOM', a whole side wall of stalactites were instantly obliterated, the chamber itself rattling for dear life.

Each turning to look at the other, after a few moments, the deafening silence was pierced by howling roars of laughter. Josh collapsed to the floor, while his brother's resounding tones of mirth resounded around the walls.

After wiping the frozen tears from his face, Josh turned to his sibling and said,

"That was brilliant. Best day ever!"

Man's huge jaw nodded in agreement as the sound of approaching footsteps brought them down to earth with a bump.

"I think you'd better change back," remarked Josh nervously.

Man did just that, his naked human form quickly slipping into his newly found rags.

As some of their father's men came sprinting around

the corner in front of them, the two boys just stood there, shell-shocked.

Drawing to a halt directly in front of them, the one in charge glared before asking,

"What was that noise?"

As Josh quivered next to him, Man's quick thinking brain had no trouble answering the question.

"Rock fall, over there," he pointed in the same direction as the fireball had headed off in.

"Anyone hurt?" enquired the guard.

"There was nobody here but us."

"Well... that's something," declared the guard, instantly relieved. "I'll let your father know. We might have to cordon off that part of the chamber. I should get going, just in case there are any aftershocks."

Neither of them needed to be told twice, both dashing off in the direction the guards had come from.

Elsewhere in the compound, the leader had shown their serpent-like guest to a small, remote enclosure in the coldest depths of their prison. For his part, the naga seemed to relish the ice and frost. As he vowed to try his hardest to get in touch with his king, Man's father told him he'd post a guard outside for when he was finished. Marg's first instinct was to thank his host for his generosity, something the leader found greatly amusing, deep inside his head anyway, on the walk back to his quarters.

Once there, he rounded up all of the males, excluding all the youngsters, and began to lay out his plan. The rudimentary weapons that they had stored for such an occasion were to come out of hiding and be readily available. A large contingent of their force were told to stay within sight of Marg at all times, ready to take him down at a moment's notice. Each and every one of them knew that he had to be taken alive. Killing him made them weak. As their captive, he could be bargained for and much, much more. Understanding their orders, they headed off, determined to get as close as they could, while looking as though they were going about their daily business. Stealth was needed now, more than ever. Plans were drawn up, contingencies made should the king of the nagas come to investigate what on earth was going on. Through the cutting cold of the ice that pierced their lungs in agony every time they breathed, hope slowly started to seep back into those that knew exactly what was going on. They stood up straighter, carried themselves with that much more composure, occasionally letting a smile play out across their rugged and timeworn features, when there was no one watching.

In their mother's cramped and compact living area, Josh was busy spouting on about his brother's transformation into a real life dragon, with all the enthusiasm he could muster. Astounded, their mother turned to her oldest son for confirmation.

"It's true... everything he's said."

All she could do was look on in disbelief.

"And you say that this naga creature is still here?"

"As far as I know, it is. As Father's guest if I'm not mistaken."

A noticeable frown crept across the ravaged features of her face on hearing this.

"What is it?" asked Man, as politely as he could.

"It's nothing," she whispered.

"Clearly it's something... tell us, please."

"From what I know," she whispered, glancing around to make sure no one other than her sons was listening, "the nagas are one of the ancient races, one of the only ones to be left out of signing the ancient agreement, the one related to the famed prophecy the dragon domain is so keen on invoking, whenever they get the chance."

"Why does that matter?" asked Josh.

Their mother, head bowed, was clearly thinking carefully about her next words.

"My understanding is, at the time, they as a race were considered too naive and gullible to be part of the proceedings. The worry was that they would somehow become compromised, thus endangering the whole deal. I don't know whether that's true or not, or whether the nagas as a race have changed across the centuries. All that I've ever heard about them, is that after being excluded from everything in and around the prophecy and the agreement, they went into some kind of self-imposed exile. If they are still as trusting and easy to fleece as ever, then I would think, even as we speak, plans are underway to take advantage of that."

By this time, tears had started to well up in her eyes, a cool, flat, frosting coating the frozen liquid. With her dirty, drawn out nails, she chipped away the slivers of ice, watching them fall carelessly to the floor.

"I don't understand," interjected Man. "Why don't we just ask for the nagas' help, instead of plotting to take advantage of them? Surely that's easier and fits in more comfortably with the plan that we already have?"

Holding her head in her hands, it was then that a decision had to be made. For too long she'd kept them in the dark about what was really going on, tried to maintain their innocence. It looked very much as though the time had come to let it all out.

Both brothers knew that a tipping point had been reached, but not why, how or even what about. Their reasonably short lives were about to be changed forever.

"I don't think your father has been entirely honest with you about the plan," sniffed their mother, terrified that this moment had finally arrived.

"I don't understand," murmured Man softly.

Here and now, Josh was almost a bystander.

"I'm pretty sure you only know part of the plan."

"And which part would that be?" asked the elder of the

two.

"On becoming trapped here, those of us left alive were rightly outraged at what had been done to us. After a few fruitless decades of trying to escape, your father and a few others came up with something long term that they thought just might work."

Both boys bowed their heads in shame. Of course they knew exactly what she was talking about: procreating in their human forms in an effort to continue their genetic bloodlines and just maybe find some spark of magic that could survive in this hostile environment. Because only a handful of females had survived their original incarceration, and after a long process of manipulating their DNA into exact human replicas, it was decided by those in charge, in particular their leader, that all of the males would have access to all of the females, all of the time. It was brutal, hedonistic and despicable for each and every one of the females. Supposedly though, it was a just cause, at least that's what they'd been led to believe. But the fact that it was still going on in some way, shape or form, just proved how very wrong it was. That, as far as they understood it, was THE PLAN!

Being a kind, thoughtful, intelligent soul, and of course a fantastic mother in the circumstances, she could see the confusion raging in their eyes. Although she'd dreaded this day coming for some time now, a sense of relief at the truth finally getting out removed a huge weight off her shoulders.

"We thought this was it," chipped in Josh, keen to do his part. "We were born," he ventured, skipping over the desperate and evil acts that had been done to get to that part, "and were supposed to nurture the very different magic that was thought to be inside us. That in itself was believed to be enough to get us out of here, because it was hoped that we might have gained some resistance to the cold and that any ethereal power contained within us might be more than enough to facilitate an escape."

"Now though, you're telling us there's more to it than that?" questioned Man.

Their mother nodded her head, her breathing shallow, her face looking sunken and broken.

"While, as far as I know, that was part of the plan, it certainly wasn't all of it. I think those in a position of power calculated that, at some point, some being or other would stumble across us. It was unlikely, but given the amount of time we'd been here, and would be here, the odds narrowed dramatically. From what I can gather, preparations were made for such an eventuality. If I had to guess, I would say that they're being enacted, right at this very moment."

"And that involves what exactly?" demanded Josh, a little too harshly.

Man laid his hand on his brother's shoulder, urging him to calm down. Instantly he regretted his tone of voice and apologised.

"So they're going to take advantage of the naga's gullibility, is that it?"

Exhaling whilst shaking her head, her mother didn't really want to go any further. But the cat was out of the bag, and as was its wont, it most certainly wasn't going to go back in.

"Please Mother," urged Man. "Tell us what's happening."

"I think 'take advantage of' would probably be something of an understatement," was all that she could say.

Both brothers shared a look, exchanging unspoken words in just a glance.

"Surely it would be best for everybody concerned if we just asked for their help, perhaps in exchange for some knowledge we have or even a chance to work off our debt with them?" remarked Josh, eagerly.

"I don't think anyone here sees it that way, least of all your father."

After a few moments of tense silence, Man spoke up.

"What are they going to do?"

"Honestly," replied his mother, "I don't know. But nothing good, that's for sure."

"Whatever it is, I bet they'll need my help," declared Man angrily. "And I won't give it to them."

Josh slapped his brother on the arm playfully before declaring,

"We need to leave... you have to help!"

"I have to do no such thing. I want no part in harming another race. Our freedom is not worth hurting beings looking only to befriend us."

"But..."

"No ifs, no buts... I simply won't be part of it!"

With their mother in the middle, both brothers glared ferociously at each other, each believing they were on the right side of the argument. It was the first time in living memory that they'd ever properly fallen out. And it could have major repercussions.

Unbelievably, the atmosphere around the three of them became frostier than ever.

Hundreds of miles away in the ice cold water of the Southern Ocean, a slick, sleek, silver shape rolled through the foaming break of two metre high waves, tossing and turning, diving down and rocketing back up through the current, thrilled at being out here alone, not at any point remembering her vow to meet up with the rest of her kind. As the wickedly chilly water oxygenated her gills, something attracted her consciousness, a kind of knock, knock, knocking on the door. Assuming that once again she'd lost all concept of time and had overstayed her welcome in these remote and exhilarating waters, she answered the call, as that's what it was, wondering not for the first time in recent history just what her punishment would be.

"Uh... hello?" she uttered, recognising the touch of one of her own.

"Who's this?"

"My name is Welwyn. Who are you?"

"I'm Marg, and I need your help. I don't have long, so please listen carefully."

"Sure thing."

"I'm lost inside the Antarctic shelf."

"Do you want me to come and find you? I can be there within a few hours."

"That's a very nice offer, but not really relevant under the circumstances. I've stumbled across something, something important... a community of disavowed dragons, who have news of a diabolical plot by those in the dragon domain, one that would wipe out all of the ancient races, including us."

"Oh my!"

"I need you to get a message to the monarch. He needs to come here and see this, NOW!"

And with that, he passed on all the information he could to the young naga known as Welwyn. For her part, she promised to get the message to the king. Before communication was cut off for good, Marg managed to send her the estimated coordinates of the dark, foreboding entrance that had started his unbelievable journey. Abruptly contact was cut. Exhausted, he coiled up on the floor, the cold from the ice refreshing nearly all of him. Thoughts of being rewarded by the king of their race for the part he'd played in uncovering this underhand plot raced through his head. Little did he know it could lead to the downfall of his kind.

With his men in place, all he had to do now was wait, something he wasn't good at and didn't relish, but having waited all these decades to get to this point, he supposed it wasn't so much of a hardship. Tapping his fingers on the frost covered wall, his mind raced back to where it had all come apart, his feelings for the being that had captured him stalking to the surface, making his arms quiver, setting free more goose bumps than usual.

'That damn city. If only I hadn't stopped there. Of course it had seemed like a good idea at the time, having drawn him out from his allies, sure that he would be no match for someone as clever as me, particularly as he'd chosen to stay in that dreaded human form, just to appease those all around him. I knew he'd do that... in the city at least. I should have taken him down, should have finished it there and then. How on earth did it go so wrong?'

Memories of the shattered portcullis splintering all around him as terrorised citizens, scared for their lives, just as they should be, fled on foot in every different direction. It brought a smile to his face, even after all this time, even in this tragic hellhole of a place. He could, and perhaps should have flown on, but making a stand there seemed like the logical thing to do, especially given the injury to the brachialis muscles that connected his body and wings. Painful couldn't do justice to what it was he felt when flying. It took all his magic and dominant will to block out the explosive feelings of hurt. Landing had been a joy, but a curse as well. As soon as his nemesis turned up in that ridiculous suit of armour, it was obvious he'd once again have to take to the air, something he really didn't want to do. It would, however, be worth it, to be rid of him once and for all. A brief wave of euphoria washed over him as the memory of belting out brilliant streams of bright orange flame in all directions, incinerating people, buildings and surfaces in every direction. Just the thought of killing on that scale perked him right up. And then HE had turned up, ruining it all. Inevitable, most would say, but not him though. Why they'd ever formed a friendship in the first place, was totally beyond his comprehension.

Fleeting encounters had occurred over the next few minutes, with the knight's armour, and moreover his shield, taking the full force of the ferocious flame that had blackened the protective covering in numerous places. A standoff ensued, in front of what remained of the city, with all the denizens watching in fascination. It was at that exact moment, he could remember having to stifle a laugh. That idiot ex-friend of his, started, unbelievably, to remove all of his remaining armour. What the hell? Looking on in disbelief, he remembered having absolutely no idea what was happening. His first thought was that it was a distraction, and it wouldn't have been the first time, perhaps to buy his allies a small amount of time to arrive. But it wasn't that... he would have sensed them, and they were nowhere nearby.

With the armour stripped off, and his shield discarded on the cobbles off to his right, the idiot then appeared to play to the crowd, weaving the heavy sword about his body, using a touch of the magic they both knew he had, the dull metallic blade now a blur to all of those watching.

'All of those but me, that is.' Knowing that the moment was at hand, and that not even fate could prevent the inevitable confrontation, one of them would most certainly perish over the next few seconds. And without any doubt, he knew that it wouldn't be him.

Watching on as his former comrade in arms silently mouthed the words, "Let's do it!", he felt absolutely no remorse for what was to come as his opponent took off in a charge directly towards him. Ignoring the excruciating agony from his injured muscles, with one bound from his mighty legs he took to the air, the feeling of the wind rushing over both sides of his wings as satisfying as it had ever been. With one gigantic flap, the four hundred metre gap closed to almost nothing as stone, wood, dust and broken bodies whipped up in the air behind him. With the eyes of every inhabitant of the city on him, he vowed to finish them all off to a man and a woman, after he'd dealt with his adversary. As time slowed, he let out the most humungous cone of flame directly in front of him, intent on incinerating his nemesis once and for all. For all intents and purposes, there appeared absolutely no way out, and that he'd won. As the inevitable drew closer, for a split second he lost sight of the being he hated most in this world, the one that had been assigned to hunt him down. Expecting to see the burnt crisp of human remains, he was stunned to see his enemy pour on more speed, and then disappear beneath his thunderous, roaring cone of flame.

After that, things were just a blur. The idea of circling around to have another go was short lived, as an intense pain shattered the scales around his belly, sending a continuous wave of agony up into his major organs. All thought of flight was forgotten as he crashed unceremoniously to the ground. After that, it was all very hazy, tiny snippets appearing and disappearing at once. People watching him from afar as he lay helpless on the shattered cobbles of the city, too afraid to come any closer, as the tang of magic hung in the air. Movement, he could remember being moved, but not where or how. And then of course there was arriving in the domain, in front of all of those dragon lackeys, so keen to support their beloved king, so keen to do the right thing, so keen to look after their human pets. Whatever magic that demented old dragon had used on him to turn him into his human persona hurt like hell, of that much he was sure. As he defiantly turned around, imprisoned by the supernatural, he caught a familiar face out of the corner of one eye. As a knowing wink passed between them, it was at that point that he comprehended he'd get another chance, that it wasn't all over and that he and his followers would live to prevail another day. After that, his memories became more than a little foggy, at least for a while anyway.

Momentarily, his fingers stopped tapping against the wall as a surge of rage and frustration built up inside him. Only then did the final memories come back to him. On waking, he could vividly remember the feeling of flying, only it must have been a dream, he thought, because he was stuck in his abhorrent human guise. It took a few moments to realise the reality of things, and only then did the true horror of his situation strike home. He was being transported with others around him, beneath a dragon body, huge wings flailing out above him on either side. Using all his force of will, he struggled, but to no avail. Instead of tapping the wall, he smashed his fist against the rock and ice, letting out a yell of pain on contact, the blood trickling from the freshly opened wounds. Still he was stuck in the past.

Cold, he felt a pure, evil cold piercing every atom of his body. It was then that he knew what was going on. They were transporting them to the site in Antarctica, the one the dragon scientists had stumbled upon completely by accident all those years ago. That was to be their punishment: death, eventually, by cold. Every sinew in his body rebelled at the very thought of where they were going, and what would happen after they arrived. By the time the others knew what was going on, it would be all over. Searching frantically for his magic, he realised that like those captives all around him, somehow it had been contained. Frustrated and frightened out of his mind, it was then that he remembered Osvaldo winking at him during his so-called trial. Once again, hope sprang up.

'He must have done something to aid us in our time of need, but what?'

As the frost nibbled at his extremities, the realisation that they'd nearly arrived at their destination struck him like a sledgehammer. It was exactly then that, out of the blue, his magic returned. Mouthing Osvaldo a silent thank you, he broke free of the restraints that had bound him in place, and as he dropped like a stone, unlocked the bonds inside his DNA, enabling the change within him to start taking place, much as others around him were doing. Freefalling into the darkness, for a brief moment it looked as though death were a certainty. But as the magic and his temper raged, his natural form took hold, and with all the skill of a dragon twice his age, he pulled up and out of a death defying dive if ever there was one, and headed up and back into the mother of all battles. Striking this way and that, it was hard to access the magic within. So instead, he used his mighty prehistoric frame to take as many of his enemies down as possible. Raking wings with his razor sharp talons, he butted heads, spewed brilliant jets of red hot fire and caught others unaware with his mighty tail. It was at that point, amidst all the chaos, that he caught sight of a dragon carrying an array of electrical equipment. It took him a few moments to work it out, but eventually he got it.

'They're watching!'

That was all the motivation he needed. Doubling back around on himself, powered by his gigantic, matt black wings, he headed for the nearest dragon encumbered by the strength-sapping weight of all of the equipment. A pale looking creature, with flecks of different colour running consistently up its back and tail, briefly it faced the other way, unaware of the deadly threat heading towards it at speed, its mind still focusing on the job at hand, to capture the images of what was going on for the king and council. Overcome by fury and thunder, he could remember the focal point of his ire being the dragon's long and slender neck. Slamming on the brakes by stretching out his wings and flexing them upwards, his wide opened jaws arrived perfectly either side of the neck that he'd been aiming for. With a bite force unparalleled across the planet, he closed his jaws with as much satisfaction as he could ever remember, savouring the bright green blood dribbling into his mouth. As the two separate pieces of the dragon's body spiralled down towards the darkness, a very different kind of darkness encompassed his very soul. Madness and evil intertwined, filling him with a twisted vision of the future, forcing a crazed look of malevolence to become etched onto the prehistoric features of his face. Only at that singular moment did he realise the trouble he was in.

There was another dragon sending images back to the domain, and it was further back down the tunnel that had obviously led them here. Lurching forward with all his might, he started to give chase, but his target had a considerable lead on him and had already figured out that it was time to leave. It was then that an overwhelming sense of danger shot through him, tickling his threat sense, forcing him to glide to a halt. Issuing a call to all his remaining followers to fall back into the brightly lit cavern, reluctantly they did so, leaving the remaining enemy force to limp back down the all encompassing tunnel. At that exact moment, the first of the charges went off, collapsing the cavernous ceiling directly in front of them. As a group, they fled further back inside the cavern, all the time accompanied by the deafening noise of more charges exploding in the distance, the realisation that they were well and truly trapped, only now dawning.

As blood dribbled from the knuckles on his right fist, tears froze just below his eyes, so powerful were the memories of his incarceration. Vowing there and then to exact revenge not only on the incompetent Osvaldo, the current dragon monarch, whoever that should be, (boy, was that going to be interesting), but the dragon domain as a whole, he rolled up all of his hope and compartmentalised it just like he'd been taught to do, all that time ago. They would escape this place, and when they did, there would be hell to pay.

"Please can you take me to your leader?" asked the naga from within the remote enclosure.

Nodding in agreement, knowing that his boss would want to see the despicable creature as soon as possible, the guard led the way through the freezing cold compound, determined not to look in the direction of all the others milling about in their immediate vicinity.

It was effectively night time, although nobody within

the frosty prison actually knew for sure. Not long after their confinement, it had been decided to set their own day and night hours, so that everybody knew where they were even though it probably didn't match what was going on in the outside world, somewhere far above them.

Nearly asleep in his chair, the blood from the gash on his fingers from having thumped the wall, soaked up by one long, twisted, dirty rag, wrapped tightly around his hand, the slightest movement in the doorway to his room snapped him back to reality in an instant.

"Sorry," declared the guard, aware of having woken up their leader.

"What is it?"

"Our guest here has finished his task and wanted to update you on his progress."

Deep within Man's father's mind, fireworks were exploding, a sense of fulfilment and joy resounded off every dark corner. Surely it had worked, was all that he could think.

"Do send him in, do send him in."

Through the dull lit passageway, sliding silently across the floor, Marg slithered in through the doorway, slipping to a halt directly in front of the leader.

Sensibly, and not wanting to get his hopes up more than they already were, the leader decided to wait and see what kind of progress their guest had made. As it happened, quite a lot.

"I managed to contact one of my kind on the outer limits of my telepathic reach," announced the serpent-like beast.

"Impressive," ventured Man's father, pouring on the charm.

"Thank you. I asked that she contact the king, and get him to come to us as soon as possible. It should be done, but how long it takes could be anybody's guess. Days probably, maybe even weeks... it all depends on where the monarch currently resides. As you know, we, as a race, lead a nomadic existence, not staying in any one place too long. He could be anywhere in the southern hemisphere."

Although not thrilled to hear all this, the fact that the message had gotten out, pleased him immeasurably. All they had to do now was bide their time, and then the endgame could begin. Slowly, the pieces of the puzzle were falling into place.

The following day Man awoke normally, pleased that his brother was nowhere to be seen. After a meagre breakfast of raw vegetables on the run, the elder of the two brothers ground to a halt next to a fruitful patch of recently grown food in one of the hydroponics bays. Filling one of the huge sacks lying on the ground, he plodded off in the direction of Unlucky, determined to fulfil his duty to the best of his ability, hoping that he wouldn't bump into his sibling along the way.

Strolling purposefully around the corner, Man arrived at the haggard detainee, instantly aware of two things. There was no sign of his brother, and that the defenceless prisoner once again sported mysterious injuries, this time across both of his wings.

"I see you've managed to hurt yourself again... that's quite some talent you have, particularly given your bindings."

Unlucky's gaze remained firmly on the white permafrost floor, hardly noticing the new arrival at all.

"What's going on?" asked Man softly, sensing something was amiss, but not really having any idea as to what.

Still nothing.

"Fine! Don't talk to me then. I go out of my way to make sure you're fed, stop my brother from taking out his anger on you, and this is the way you pay me back. Perhaps I should stop coming altogether. Is that what you want?"

Sluggishly, Unlucky lifted up his gigantic prehistoric skull to meet Man's gaze head on.

"Do you really expect me to believe that you don't know what's going on?"

"What do you mean? I have absolutely no clue as to what you're talking about. Now please, tell me what's been happening."

Willing away the pervasive agony from not only the fresh injuries, but the others that he'd sustained night after night for some time now, Unlucky, as he'd become known by the two boys, had to think more than twice about revealing the truth as he knew it. Realising he could pay dearly for speaking his mind, he wanted nothing more than to set the truth free.

"You are a very naive young... I nearly said human, but of course you're a dragon."

"Why am I naive?" he asked aggressively, some of his anger from the previous nights events shining through.

"You come to feed me every morning, and yet only on a couple of occasions have you noted my injuries... injuries that if you thought about it for just a moment, you'd realise I couldn't possibly inflict on myself. Naive sounds about right, don't you think?"

Swallowing down his anger, Man thought about what the dragon prisoner had said for a few moments, trying to get his head around everything that was going on. Just like the conversation with his mother and brother only a few hours earlier, he really didn't like where this was all going.

"If not by your own hand, how did the injuries occur?"

Letting out a huge freezing breath that clearly caused him an awesome amount of pain, and resigned to his fate, Unlucky continued.

"Your... father pays me a visit almost every night. We have what he likes to call... a little 'chat'. After which he normally takes out more than a little of his frustration."

Man was aghast.

"How long has this been going on?"

Shaking his huge dinosaur-like jaw, this way and that, it was all Unlucky could do to hold on to the question in his tortured brain.

"Uhhh... some time now I suppose. Time here seems immeasurable."

Man knew exactly what the trapped prisoner meant. The passing of time in this godforsaken place had no meaning whatsoever. Seconds could be minutes, days could be weeks. Months blended seamlessly into years. Nothing was as it appeared in this hope-crushing confinement.

Rubbing his forehead with his fingers in an effort to stave off the cold, a small, hidden part of him reached out, squeaking that it knew all along what had been going on. Had he known? It didn't seem like he did. Perhaps deep down though, his subconscious knew. If that were the case, that made him complicit in what had been going on... wanton torture and cruelty.

Dropping the sack of food he wrenched his head back as far as it would go, and facing the ceiling let out the loudest cry that he could. Rocks shook, snow fell, as wickedly spreading cracks appeared in the ice across the floor.

Frustration, rage, fury and anger fought for dominance within the youngster at the dastardly deeds going on all around him. What had happened to his mother all that time ago, something no one seemed comfortable in mentioning, no one comfortable in calling it what it was... RAPE! Still going on, even now, even when supposedly there was no need, it could no longer be classed as part of the plan and a necessity. Acts of violence carried out in the dead of night against a bound and helpless prisoner.

'Surely we're better than that?' he thought.

And then there was the underlying plan, to subvert the naga and any of his kind and... do what? Force them to do their bidding? How on earth would that work? He had absolutely no idea, but after the awkward conversation last night, he had little doubt that's what was going to happen. And so here he was, stuck in indecision, mired in a pickle, caught in a conundrum, the morals inside him tested to their full extent, unable to foresee a way out for any of them.

Out of nowhere, he felt drained, let down, lifeless. Letting himself go, he slumped to the floor, the tattered, filthy rags acting as trousers taking the brunt of it as his arse slammed down on the ground. Head in hands, for the very first time in his life he felt lost and alone, a creature out of place, surrounded by darkness and unnecessary evil.

"I'm sorry to add to your burden," submitted Unlucky, softly. "You seem like an honest being, full of honour, unlike most around here. And to answer your question, I am grateful that you come to feed me every day, even though sometimes it may appear otherwise."

Of all the beings trapped here below the ice, the two he found most relatable at the moment were the bound and chained dragon, a relic from their original incarceration, and the newly arrived visitor, a member of a totally different race. How had it come to this?

"There seems to be more than just this troubling you. Is it to do with finding your magic and the stunning transformation that you undertook yesterday?"

Somewhere inside him, a voice shouted out that he'd already said too much, and that to reveal any more would be an act of treason, something he'd be unable to undo. But whether because of how truly lost and alone he felt, or because he was desperate for some sort of guidance, he unwisely ploughed on, realising that he'd reached some kind of tipping point, one that could either plunge him deep into the darkness, or fill him full of light. More than anything, he needed another being's opinion.

"The women here were raped, over and over again. That's how we were created," he blurted, a sense of guilt rushing over him at having been born out of that.

Waving his head through the frost filled air, flexing his

degrading muscles as much as his bonds would allow, Unlucky answered with as much kindness as he could muster.

"Although I didn't know for sure, I figured as much."

"How can beings do such a thing to other beings? It makes no sense at all."

"Dark deeds can be born out of necessity, frustration, hidden agendas and of course good intentions. Without knowing all the details, it would be impossible for me to comment any further."

"As if that weren't enough, I find the torture of a prisoner to be a regular undertaking as well as…"

Silence hung like the cold in the air between the two of them. Maybe this was a step too far.

"There's something else, on top of what you've already told me?"

Not wanting to repeat what his mother had told them last night, especially given it could be tortured out of the dragon prisoner by his father on his next visit, Man decided there and then to stay quiet. But it was never going to be that easy. Although only having been a guard, doing his duty for his monarch and the dragon domain as a whole, Unlucky, much like every other dragon in his position, was quick witted and smart, something he'd kept hidden for nearly all of his incarceration, figuring it would get him into more trouble, hoping to prolong his stay, just in case a rescue attempt was in the offing. He had, however, long since given up on that happening. Here and now though, his intellect and inquisitiveness was positively shining through.

"There's something going on with the naga, isn't there?" he asked.

Inside his mind, Man cursed loudly at having given the game away. Denial seemed a complete waste of time now.

"They're planning to use him somehow. I don't know all the details."

Unlucky pondered what he'd just been told for a few

moments.

"I would have thought they wouldn't stand a chance. Nagas are formidable warriors with a vast array of unusually tainted magic. I'd bet my life on the fact that the single being who arrived here out of nowhere, could with little or no trouble, take out the entire underground frozen realm and everyone within it. What you say makes no sense."

"Something's afoot, of that I'm sure."

"Have they asked you to be part of it?"

"What do you mean?"

"You're the only one amongst them, the only one here other than the naga, that can access even a semblance of their magic. You might be the difference between winning and losing."

"I haven't been asked, and I won't help them."

"That sounds like the right thing to do, but how strong is the courage of your convictions?"

"What's that supposed to mean?"

"Only that your leader, and father, is much more cunning than anyone gives him credit for. I'd be surprised if he hasn't planned for every eventuality."

This gave Man more than a little cause for concern. Considering everything he knew, Unlucky seemed to have hit the nail on the head. From the very first second of all this happening, his father had been one step in front of them all. If that were the case now, what did that mean for..."

One thought, and one thought only popped directly into the front of his head. Instantly he knew how he'd do it. Kicking the overflowing sack of food off in Unlucky's direction, Man whirled around and hurried off in the direction of the female quarters, with but one objective... to get to his mother, as quickly as possible.

Without any airs or graces, Man charged into the

women's block, shouting for those in front of him to move out of the way. They did so, albeit reluctantly. Turning the sharp corner into his mother's tiny space, he wasn't totally surprised to find it empty. Glancing around for any sign that she'd been here recently, and more importantly, to see if there was any sign that she'd be coming back sometime soon, it was then that he noticed the marks on the floor. Beings had been here, not too long ago, and more than one, he thought. As well, there were clear marks in the ice where someone had been dragged away, against their will.

'Oh Mother,' he thought, as his mind turned over and over what could possibly have happened. Rallying against doing anything rash, instinctively he cast those thoughts aside as the magic within him welled up inside. He had power now, real touchable, usable power, something that he could hold over others, in an effort to demand his mother's release. They wouldn't defy him, not even his father. As far as he was concerned, he had the power and justification for what he needed to do. And so with that, he turned and very deliberately stomped off in the direction of the leader's room, heading for the mother (get it?!) of all confrontations.

On their leader's orders, the remote enclosure that the naga had used for peace and solitude in an effort to contact his brethren, had been turned into a basic refuge for him, and very pleased he was about it, constantly thanking those in the immediate vicinity, more than really needed to be there. It was a good job he wasn't paying too much attention, or his mind might have asked why there were so many, and just what were they all up to? Thankfully, for the leader at least, he didn't. Almost the furthest point away from the dragon prisoner, and more importantly, the entrance point to the submerged stream, the only real way out of the frosty confinement they all found themselves in, nearly the whole of their fighting force sat between the naga and the only way out, again something he hadn't really considered.

Arriving at the outer reaches of his father's accommodation, he was surprised to see the guards move aside with such ease. Clearly he was expected. Plucking up all the courage he could muster, and with his face as neutral as he could make it, he marched full throttle around the corner, determined to take control of what would happen next. Little did he know what was playing out around him.

Father facing away, leaning down and fiddling with something unseen, he draw silently to a halt, barely able to contain the rage he felt inside.

"Ahhh... if it isn't my prodigy? What fine timing. I was just coming to ask you for your help."

As the leader turned and stood up to his full height, Man got a sense of something else going on, although he wasn't quite sure what.

"You are going to give me your undivided loyalty and help... aren't you?"

Swallowing nervously, alone and afraid apart from the anger and fear pumping through his veins, he remembered what had been done, and that in itself stoked his decision making.

"NO... I won't help!"

"Hmmmm... I'm shocked."

That wasn't the reaction from his father that he'd been expecting.

"What have you done with her?"

"Ahhh yes, your mother. I thought she might come in handy."

"For what?"

"To persuade you in your wisdom to do the right thing and help out your brethren."

"Why would you think I needed persuading?"

From a small dark space, adjacent to an icy corner that he'd never spotted before, out stepped his brother, head bowed, unable to look him in the eyes."

One word and one word alone popped up inside Man's highly functioning brain.

"TRAITOR!"

"Some here still have morals and family values."

"DON'T YOU DARE TALK TO ME ABOUT FAMILY VALUES AFTER EVERYTHING YOU'VE DONE! AND AS FOR HIM, BETRAYING HIS MOTHER LIKE THAT, THE TWO OF YOU CLEARLY BELONG TOGETHER!"

"Done in the name of survival, to see all of us through this, out the other side in an attempt to escape this prison and take our rightful places back in the real world."

"You can justify it however you like, but it's still wrong, something you're acutely aware of."

"My, my... aren't you a wise old head on very young shoulders. I'll ask you once again. Are you going to help? Think very carefully about your answer."

Not missing for one moment the menace and threat behind the words, he knew in his heart of hearts that he couldn't help with whatever dastardly plan his father had that involved the nagas. It went against everything he believed in, and there was nothing he could or would say that might change his mind. Words, however, were not the leader's strong suit. Actions were.

"I'd say it's a shame that it's come to this... but I can't really say that I'm surprised. You always were a bit of a softy. But now you get to choose what happens next."

From alongside his father, another concealed entrance that he hadn't known about revealed itself, as two bulky men, one either side of his mother, marched out, both carrying glisteningly sharp stalactites, one only millimetres away from his mother's throat. The fear and terror in her eyes were there for everyone to see.

The very first thought to enter his brain, was whether or not he could cross the distance between them and disarm both, before they could do her any harm. Instantly he dismissed it as impossible. But just maybe there was something he could do. Tired, scared, fed up and utterly ashamed, delving inside himself, he yanked on the magic, forcing it up into his limbs, ready to dispense it at will.

Out of nowhere, bright light and the most violent pain he'd ever felt erupted from the middle of his back, dropping him to his knees, forcing him to cry out in pain.

"MAN!" screamed his mother, trying to break free from the vice-like grip her attackers had on her.

Through the existential agony he could just make out the stuttering power inside him that had started to flicker away. It was now or never. Reaching out to grasp it and end everything playing out around him, a huge 'CRACK' tore through the room. Milliseconds later he realised that the sound had been his right kneecap splintering into a dozen pieces. Unable to catch his breath, even enough to shout out in pain, as the beating continued, he watched his mother's attempt to break free and reach him. Of course she couldn't. Curled up in a ball, constantly battered by metal wielding thugs on either side of him, the ethereal power he'd sought to bring forth had disappeared off into the wilderness of his mind, hardly a hint of where it had gone remaining. Watched by his father, brother, struggling mother and the two handing out the beating, the violence subsided after an instruction from his father, a minute or so later. Having recognised what the boy was about to do, the leader had handled it in the only way he knew how, and had overcome his son's newly found magical abilities.

As bright red, viscous blood pooled in the ice on the floor all around him, still curled up in the foetal position, Man whimpered and cried, sniffled and sobbed. It was an unbecoming sight for someone with so much power.

"Not so wise it would appear, after all," scoffed their father from across the room. The words had no effect on his son, even if he had heard them.

"LET HIM GO!" bellowed his mother, still desperately trying to break free in an effort to reach her boy, still without any luck.

Two strides, and instantly the leader found himself standing in front of the boy's mother.

"NO!" he screamed in her face, before drawing back his arm and punching her full in the nose, blood, bone and cartilage spraying the wall behind her.

Josh jumped up, or at least in his mind did, but that's all it was... a fantasy. In reality he stayed locked in place, far too scared to act, all too aware of the price caused by the decision he'd made.

Grabbing the boy's mother by the throat, a deep seated pleasure at the sight of what he'd done to her coursing through his body, very dispassionately the leader spoke.

"You're mine, BITCH, to do with as I please. You always were and you always will be. Don't ever forget that."

From his position on the floor, Man could see what was happening and just make out the words. There and then, reality hit hard, driving home the precise order of things.

"Let her go," he coughed from the ground, blood oozing through wobbly teeth before falling precariously to the cold encrusted floor.

"NO!" yelled his father.

"I'll do it! Whatever you want. Just let her go."

Letting go of the woman's throat, the leader turned around to face his battered and bloody son.

"She stays safe with me until this is all over. After you've played your part, she'll be returned... you have my word."

Man knew there and then, that it was the best deal he was going to get, and although comprehending that his father's word could never be trusted, he nodded his head in agreement, despite the reservations he had. With his brother having betrayed him, getting them all into this in the first place, his overwhelming sense of duty, loyalty and passion resided very much with his mother. She was all he had now, and he'd do anything to keep her safe. Slowly, he sat up, waves of pain surging through his body as he did so.

Noticing his son's discomfort, the leader smiled as he spoke.

"I would suggest you use your gift to heal up. You need to be up and ready, starting tomorrow."

"To do what, exactly?"

"You'll befriend our guest, stay with him at all times, apart from when he's resting."

"To what aim?"

"Hopefully he can help you unlock the secrets to your powers, maybe even teach you some more magic. Act reluctant at first, almost as though it's him giving you the ideas. Gobble up as much of it as you can, especially anything offensive. You may well need that at a later date."

"What if he doesn't want to teach me anything?"

"Then I suggest you use all of your skills to get him to do just that. It would be a shame if anything were to happen to your mother whilst you were away."

Not even a thinly veiled threat, Man knew.

"If I can get that far, what then?"

"Under no circumstances is he allowed to leave. He's that far from the stream for a reason. Should he look as though that's what's happening, you are to warn my men. Do you understand?"

Man knew a command when he saw one.

"I do."

"Good. Make sure you do, otherwise there'll be hell to pay."

"And then that's it... she's free to go, and will be left undisturbed?"

"To a point. When more of his kind turn up, I'll have other uses for you. And you'd damn well better comply.

This is important and will secure freedom for all of us. Now go! Heal up, and first thing tomorrow, find your way to the naga and do as I've instructed."

"What about feeding the dragon prisoner?"

"Huh. Who cares?"

"He needs to be fed," quipped Man, "particularly if he's to survive more torture."

That got his father's attention. Both beings locked eyes on each other, each trying to figure out what the other was thinking. Silence reigned, apart from Man's heavy, troubled breathing.

"I see," commented his father. "This one," he said, cuffing Josh across the top of the head, will continue to feed our prisoner, although not too well. Food is a valuable commodity here and now, and I don't want it wasted on the likes of him. Is that understood?"

From a crouched position on the floor, Josh managed to grumble a, "Yes sir."

Trickling the tiniest inkling of magic into his broken knee, Man desperately tried to keep a straight face as the euphoric feeling of the power knitting the bone back together threatened to overcome him. He succeeded, but only just. Stumbling to his feet, his newly repaired knee feeling as good as new, he wiped the blood from his mouth and chin, and with one last look at his mother, turned and left, all the time cursing his father and brother.

Reaching the insignificant, tiny space that he'd always known as his, he curled up beneath the damp pile of rags that lay atop an icy block and pulled them up over his head, letting darkness shroud him. With his head still ringing, and the broken parts of his body calling out in pain, he set about putting that right. For the next few hours, he discovered almost all he could about healing... setting teeth, knitting bone, repairing skin and dampening down bruising. It was one hell of an education. Exhausted from the beating and using his magic, slumber overtook him, sending him off into a state of delirious dreaming.

Waking early, his body refreshed and fully healed from the thrashing he'd received at the hands of his father's men, Man's only, all consuming thought was for the safety of his mother. And so with that in mind, after washing briefly in the ice cold water, he set out to find his target, and follow his father's instructions. Keeping his mother safe was all that mattered.

Curled around in a huge circle on the frost bitten ground, although technically asleep, Marg could still sense the approaching life force of another. Gracefully the serpent-like beast opened one eye, and rose to full height.

"Good morning, youngster," he prompted.

"Good morning to you," Man replied, smiling profusely.

"Is there anything I can do for you?" asked the naga brightly.

'If only you knew,' thought Man, his mind focused on one singular purpose.

"I...I...I...was wondering if you could tell me about your race. Ever since you popped out of the water the other day, I've been absolutely fascinated. I hope you're not offended in any way shape or form. I'm just curious, that's all."

It was a good opening gambit, and one that Man thought just might break the ice, so to speak, metaphorically and not literally.

"Of course, of course," answered Marg keenly. "I'd only too happy to tell you all about us."

And that was how it started.

Over the course of the next few days, Man would turn up at the remote enclave Marg used as his quarters, sometime in the early morning, and the two of them would either stay there and chat, or move about the compound, with Man subtly leading him in any other direction other than that of the stream and the dragon prisoner.

At first all they talked about were his race. Feigning interest in everything their visitor had to say, he was wide-eyed in the appropriate places; using phrases such as 'wow', or 'tell me more', were regular occurrences. For his part, the naga was lured into a false sense of security, and felt as though they'd formed a reciprocal friendship. In Man's case, it was nothing more than him doing everything he could to secure his mother's freedom and safety. Getting her away from his psychotic father was the only game in town.

During the course of their discussions, Man learnt as much as he could about his new found friend's kin, figuring that at some point in the future, it might just serve him well. Marg recounted some of their history, explaining how their king at the time, and the rest of their race, felt betrayed by the Manticores and the Basilisks in the run up to the prophecy agreement. After becoming excluded through no fault of their own, a decision was taken to retreat very much out of the public eye so to speak, and return to their native regions which included the Arctic, the Southern seas and of course Antarctica. Gradually, nearly all the nagas across the planet slipped back into the water and headed for much colder climes, leaving the rest of the ancient races to govern and guide their human charges. Over the remaining centuries, nothing had really changed in that regard. Of course the Manticores and the Basilisks had gotten what was due to them. Who hadn't heard of that? Other than knowing that though, no information on anything else had been heard. Occasionally their world would collide with that of the humans, sightings of a stray vessel here, the sporadic explorer there. But these encounters were infrequent at best and not really monitored.

Explaining about their diet of fish, seal and marine mammals on day two, Man found it odd when Marg mentioned the delicious meat he'd been fed on his very first day here.

'What the...?' was all he could think. Meat, here?' In all his time, he'd never heard of such a thing. 'What was it? Where had they found it?' were the thoughts that spun throughout his head. Without thinking about it, the naga moved on.

"Of course we stay in touch via telepathy, with different clusters of us all dotted across the globe. Tiny way stations around the Equator boost communication between troupes in the southern and northern hemispheres. For the most part it works quite well, and allows us every five or ten years to visit our cousins in remote and distant waters."

"Impressive," stated Man truthfully. "What a marvellous achievement."

"We're very proud of it," declared Marg.

After that, they moved on to social conventions and the rule of law within the different groups sprinkled across the globe. It was all Man could do not to fall asleep at this point. It was a good job that he hadn't because the big payoff was about to arrive.

"And that really only leaves us with... magic!" announced Marg, knowing this would brighten up his friend's day.

It most certainly did, in more ways than one.

Hours flew by as Marg explained the basic concepts of spell weaving as he liked to call it. Excitement bubbled up deep within Man, not just at the thought of freeing his mother, but at learning ancient magic, which nobody outside the naga race had ever been taught. Seconds turned into minutes, minutes into hours, and hours into days as the two vastly different beings lost themselves in all things supernatural.

The notions at first were incredibly hard to grasp.

Whether because of the cold, their difference in nature, or because his focus was elsewhere, namely with his mother, Man struggled to perform even the most basic tasks, so much so that taking his dragon form was proving much more difficult than it had been. And that he knew was important, because if push came to shove, and Marg wanted to leave, it would almost certainly come down to him to stop him, and the only way he could do that was in the mighty, prehistoric monster guise that he thought of as his own.

Slowly, with guidance from the patient naga, who was proving to be something of a boon as a teacher, Man started to come around, began to understand some of the underpinning principles of the strange and alien spells, taking in what he'd been told, absorbing every last ounce of information. It was a revelation, and played a huge part in reinforcing his morals, or at least that's how it seemed.

On walking back to the cramped and cold place he called his own one evening, from out of nowhere appeared his father, alone and agitated, directly in his path.

"How goes it? I haven't heard from you in quite some time."

"I'm doing what you commanded, right down to the letter. If there's anything to report, then I will do, straight away."

Instantly his father took objection to his tone of voice, closing the gap between them in a matter of paces.

"You'd do well to remember who's in charge here, and just what stake you have in making sure it goes right."

"Where is she?"

"My men are... making her comfortable."

This time it was Man's turn to rally at his father's tone of voice, implying that something wholly untoward was happening.

"If she's harmed..." Man started, but a sneer from his father stopped him from going any further.

"Keep up your end of the bargain, and she'll be fine. If

you don't, or you're planning something stupid, her life will end in as much pain as possible. Make sure you remember that."

"I will."

And with that, the leader slipped off into the shadows without another word, leaving his son alone with his thoughts and machinations.

Impossible dreams haunted him nightly, causing him to convulse and wriggle, sweat and call out in what little sleep he managed to gain. In some, he and his mother had escaped this icy hellhole, living out long and productive lives in the warm countryside of some deserted island, on their own together, just the two of them. Nightmarish scenes of desperate battles with angry nagas hunting down the remaining members of their tiny community, one by one, inflicting unspeakable acts, all because of the attempted double cross by his father, forced him awake, covered in sweat, breathing heavily, scared senseless. Curling back up in an effort to get more rest, his thoughts and heart raced. Should he tell Marg exactly what was going on? On the one hand, it didn't seem like a good idea, but just maybe they could work together, save his mother and then leave this place once and for all. No doubt it would come at a cost, almost certainly the lives of many of the inhabitants, something he was more than a little reluctant to risk. But the remaining choice, the lies, betrayal and who knew what else beyond that, was killing him, eating him up inside, and went against everything he believed in. He was sure no good would ever come of it, despite what his father and the others thought.

Unable to go back to sleep, and despite the early hour, Man trudged off in the direction of Marg's enclave, wondering if it was too early to get started and whether or not at some point the naga would stop teaching him magic. Would he become bored, would it be too much of a risk, would there be certain spells that he just couldn't share? Or maybe all of the above. Deep down, he hoped that wouldn't be the case. Not only was it all absolutely fascinating, but for the first time in his life, he actually felt as though he were being treated as an adult, with respect and an appreciation for exactly what he could do. It was a fantastic feeling and one he relished, almost as much as the magic.

Plodding along the lonely path, in what would be considered the very early hours of the morning, tiny slithers of movement occasionally caught his eye. At first he thought he was imagining it, but that thought didn't last for long. Slowing to barely walking pace, feigning tiredness, throwing in the odd yawn here, the odd stretch there, he tried his best to see what was going on. Try as he might though, he couldn't get a grip on what was happening. It had to be his father, or at least his father's men, because the closer he got to Marg's quarters, the more the little oddities appeared. Only then did it strike him... he could use his magic in an effort to gain more insight.

Continuing on his way at an absolute snail's pace, he recalled everything Marg had taught him over the previous days. With barely a whisper, he called forth the supernatural power hidden deep inside him, marvelling at its touch as it flooded his subatomic bonds, momentarily setting them on fire, fuelling not only his desire but his physical body as well. In but a moment, the fatigue and exhaustion that flowed through him were washed away. Never before had he felt so alive. Careful not to show his actual feelings, and weary of the treacherous ice he was walking on, he let the magic consume him and expanded his mind, extending out the reach of his ethereal power as he did so. There... one... two... three... four... five of them, all hidden away in tiny little crevasses that he would never have known were there. It had worked, he'd found them with his magic. How good was that?!

And then it hit him, like an out of control bulldozer. If somebody as inexperienced as him, with absolutely no control over the power they wielded, could find his dad's goons, then surely Marg would have no trouble at all working out what the hell was going on. If that were the case, and he was sure that it was, what on earth should he do?

Continuing on the path at a slightly quicker pace now, not wanting anything to look out of place, his mind was alive with all the possibilities. The only certainty as far as he was concerned, was that their guest, the naga known as Marg, had to know that something was up, and if that were the case, was the truth the only way forward? Betrayal, reunion, family, blackmail, escape, were all words that popped into his head as he reached the entrance to the enclave. Swallowing nervously, he stepped around the corner, his breath freezing as he exhaled, wondering whether or not the naga was awake, and whether or not he himself was in any danger. Perhaps during the course of working together, Marg had some method of detecting his deception? Of all the thoughts running through his mind, currently, that was the one which really didn't bear thinking about.

Stealthily approaching the curled up, serpent-like monster, Man wondered exactly what he should do. If the beast was truly asleep, it might react badly to being snuck up upon. Not wishing to get any closer for fear of reprisal, he did the only thing possible in the situation... he used his magic. Finding a tiny little spark again, not wanting his actions to be mistaken for any sort of aggression, he willed it on its way towards the statue-like naga hoping to attract the attention of his mind before his body had a chance to react.

"Good morning, young one," echoed a voice deep within Man's head. "You're a little early for our lessons aren't you?"

It was disconcerting to say the least. They'd talked about this the day before, and had even made one or two half hearted attempts at doing it, but all had failed spectacularly. This though, seemed to be working a treat.

"I...I...I...I'm sorry if I startled you. That wasn't my intention."

"Sneaking up on me wasn't your intention?"

"Well, yes... but no, but... yes, but... no."

A hissing chortle, starting low but immediately getting much louder, filled every corner of his mind. It was both exciting and disturbing.

Whilst continuing to keep his mind open, Man's physical body trudged on over and slumped down next to the gigantic scaled tail, sighing as he did so.

"You seem... unhappy, youngster. Is there anything I can help you with?"

What to do, what to do?

During the course of his short life so far, Man had never found himself in anything like the quandary he was caught up in now. Right, wrong, good, bad, family, loyalty, as far as he was concerned, it all blurred together, and he struggled more than ever to get his head round all of it. Why his father couldn't just ask for their help, he really didn't know. That would have been so much easier. Instead though, he'd taken his mother hostage, threatened her with death if he didn't comply with his orders. If nothing else, he knew this to be wrong... and not just a little. This was getting out of control, too many beings' lives lay on the line. Rushing around inside him, the magic that had become the tipping point screamed out for him to do good, to follow his conscience. There and then, that's what he decided to do.

"I... I... have something to tell you. Please don't be mad," he whispered through the telepathic connection both he and Marg shared.

"Why should I be mad?"

Taking a deep breath, closing his eyes, and ignoring all of the pain from the freezing cold all around him, he replied. Doing so broke his heart.

"My father, the leader... you shouldn't trust him."

"Why on earth not?"

"They're up to something, all of them. I don't know exactly what, but if I had to guess, I'd say it involves you in some way, shape or form."

"Why are you telling me this?"

"I was tasked with gaining your trust and keeping you as far away as possible from the stream that you first arrived from, preventing you from escaping. There are others, my father's men, positioned all around, in an effort to stop you from doing the exact same thing. You must have felt them?"

"Indeed I have. It didn't take long with the power I have at my disposal. You still haven't answered my question."

"They... I mean he, he's kidnapped my mother, and is threatening to kill her if I don't do what I'm told," mumbled Man, visibly upset, even inside his mind.

Across their shared link, Marg could tell the truth was coming out and that the boy's emotions were running high. He waited to see if there was anything more.

Stoic, on the ground next to the naga's huge intimidating body, nothing outwardly appeared wrong with the leader's son and Josh's brother. Inside, things were very different, almost as though he were fighting for his life. After a long, awkward silence, the boy dragon continued.

"I didn't ask for any of this, not once. All I want to do is leave this place and lead a good life with my mother. Never have I ever harmed another being. It's not me, I just wouldn't do it."

Marg took him at his word. It seemed like the right thing to do.

"As well," continued Man, "the magic inside me... it wants me to do... good!"

'Ah,' thought the naga, 'so that's it.'

"It's quite the predicament we find ourselves in. Do you have any idea where we go from here?" asked Marg.

Trying to remain as outwardly calm as possible, he answered the only way he knew how... truthfully.

"I'm sorry... I don't. I've gone over and over it in my head, but I've no idea what to do next or just how to get out of this situation. I'd hoped by telling you the truth that somehow you just might know what to do. I fully understand if you don't want anything to do with me. I won't give away what we've said here and that you know something's up. On that you have my word."

"I don't think it'll come to that, at least I hope not for both our sakes. I would suggest we work together to formulate something in the way of a plan going forward. I don't think either of us can break free on our own, but maybe by using a little teamwork, we might just get this thing done."

"That sounds great," declared Man enthusiastically, buoyed at the thought of having someone he could trust one hundred percent on his side. "What do we do first?"

"I think we need to stay in here, act normal and proceed with your lessons. That should deflect any undue attention away from what we're doing, and hopefully hone your skills enough to help us when the chance arises to escape."

Agreeing that it was a good idea, the two of them settled down to a day's worth of magical practice. First on the agenda was setting up and breaking down a series of mental defences. So Marg explained to his young charge how to arrange the mental armour, with what force it needed to be held in place, and just what to look out for in any kind of attack or onslaught. Man did exactly as he was told. Twenty one seconds after the first practical test started, it was all over. Marg had well and truly breached his fortifications and had exacted a clear and present memory to prove that he had done so. This was how it continued over and over for the rest of the day.

By the time Man slumped down onto the familiar, cold, icy block in the insignificant space that he'd been allocated, his head hurt like hell from all the attacks that it had come up against. At first, Marg penetrated what little resistance he could offer easily. But as the day wore on, and the magic to counter the attacks was explained to him in a much more detailed way, he got better and better at dealing with the assaults, finally, right at the end, managing to oppose everything the naga had to offer, much to his amusement.

'What a day,' he thought, as his weary head and body started to succumb to the sleep that easily took him.

Overnight, having checked that the boy and the naga were both in their respective quarters and fast asleep at that, the head of the leader's force, and his trusted lieutenant, reported in, deep in the seclusion and walled off room of his boss.

"Nothing out of the ordinary appeared to be going on today. Magic was being taught, with your son struggling for the most part to pick it up, from what we could tell. They parted exhausted by the look of things, Man heading off to the room in his dorm, with our alien guest just curling up on the spot, fast asleep."

"Hmmm..."

"You're unsure of what I've told you?"

"No, not at all. It just seems a little too convenient, don't you think?"

"For all intents and purposes, it appears as though it's all going to plan."

"And that's exactly what I mean. It all appears just a little too perfect."

"Don't you think you're being a little paranoid?"

Those words from anyone else would probably have meant a severe beating, maybe even warranting a death sentence, but the second in command knew that he could speak his mind without fear. If he couldn't do that, then he couldn't do his job, and what would be the point in continuing?

"You might be right," declared the leader, after much thought. "Keep a close eye on them both. I don't trust either... not with so much at stake. All we need is a little more luck, and we'll be free. How good will that be?"

The lieutenant nodded his head eagerly, longing to be rid of this place and relaxing on a beautiful hot beach somewhere. In his mind they were already there. What could go wrong? Nothing! Everything seemed to be going to plan.

Thousands of miles away in the South Pacific Ocean, twenty one sleek, dark shapes peeled away from a group of nearly five hundred, tearing through the shadowy, harsh waters, heading south towards Antarctica, determined to find the truth behind an obscure message that had been passed between a few members of their race, implying that danger was heading their way. Little did they know, they were about to face exactly that, head on.

The very next morning in the out of the way enclave that served as Marg's room, the young boy dragon and the naga greeted each other with much pomp and circumstance, putting on a show, for those hiding discreetly out of the way. After that, it was down to business. As they both sat down, laughing and talking together, suddenly Marg launched an all out mental attack on Man, using magical brute force to batter his psychological barricades into nothing. Momentarily stunned, the leader's son responded in but a split second, repelling the attack as he had done later on yesterday, sending a surge of feedback through Marg's onslaught, catching the naga off guard, dispelling all of his unusual magic. Without appearing as though anything outwardly had happened, the guest from another domain spoke softly through their shared telepathic link, a sense of pride resonating in his voice.

"Excellent! You are a quick study. I was sure I could catch you off guard and penetrate your defences. I don't think I've ever seen reactions quite like that. You should be very proud of what you've achieved."

Catching his breath, more than a little shaken at what had just happened, again maintaining an outward facade of peacefulness and calm, he replied, all the time trying to steady himself.

"That was just a test?"

"Of course. What did you think it was?"

"I thought you were actually attacking me. I was scared for my life."

"Easy youngster... easy. It was just a test. This is how nagas learn. Their tutors constantly probe and investigate everything they've been taught, trying to catch them out, reinforcing all that they have learnt. That's all we were doing here. I wanted you to be ready, wanted to make sure you hadn't let your guard down. I suppose I could have warned you at the end of yesterday what I might try, but I wanted to see how you reacted. As tests go, you passed easily, something that bodes well for what we're trying to achieve here."

"Well... thanks, I think."

"You're welcome, my young friend. Keep up the good work, and we'll make you a formidable warrior in no time at all, and return your mother to her rightful status."

"I hope so, I truly do."

With the shock of the surprise attack out of the way, the two settled down to learn about projectile magic.

Talking out loud, Marg explained the basic principles, whilst at the same time continuing on in their bond, about a few more unusual adaptations that involved using digits... fingers to you and me, to enhance and augment the projectiles, either in power, intelligence, trajectory or doubling up, combining two or even three different forms of energy together to form a blisteringly unstoppable spell.

Fascinating didn't begin to do it justice as far as Man was concerned, and he couldn't wait to get started. The mental attacks and evasions had been an absolute revelation the previous day, but this... this was just outstanding and 'floated his boat' more than ever.

Trudging across the slippery ice, a meagre sack of spoilt vegetables and fruit slung across his shoulder, Josh, the younger of the two brothers, felt consumed by guilt at what he'd done. At the time it had seemed like the right thing to do... to go to his father and explain that Man was having second thoughts about helping them out. Now though, he was not so sure. He could never have envisaged his father taking his mother hostage, threatening her very life, in exchange for his brother's help. The look on Man's face haunted every one of his waking moments. That expression, the disappointment, the love lost, it hurt more than any of the beatings he'd taken from his father when he was younger, more than knowing what their mother had endured during her incarceration here. All he wanted was for things to go back to the way they had once been, before he'd chosen the wrong course of action. At the moment though, that seemed a million miles away.

Rounding the icy wall, his target swam into sight, looking it had to be said, more than a little worse for wear, which in itself was unusual. Getting as close as was safe to do so, Josh wondered what on earth had been going on, to see the dragon prisoner in such a state and so much pain.

"Rough night?"

Unlucky, from his frosty view point on the icy surface, just about managed to blink open one purple coloured eye, to pinpoint the source of the voice.

"What do you think?" he replied sarcastically.

"What happened?"

"What do you care?"

"I don't," mouthed Josh angrily.

"Then leave."

Incensed, Josh grabbed the bottom of the sack, and in one swift stroke, hurled the contents in the direction of the dragon prisoner, carrots, potatoes, cauliflowers, apples and oranges, most darkened, some ripped open, all landing with a 'THUD' on the floor in front of Unlucky.

Turning around, Josh started to storm off, but not before the dragon prisoner spoke up.

"Where's your brother? I haven't seen him in a few days. What's that all about?"

Much more tempestuous than his elder sibling, instantly Josh whirled around to face the cause of his immediate frustration.

"What's it to you... dragon?"

Although battered and bruised from the late night beating he'd taken only hours ago at the hands of this one's father, the prisoner held his ground, unafraid, seemingly not a care in the world, keenly aware that he'd struck a nerve. Undeterred, he ploughed on.

"I merely mention that I haven't seen him for a while. The two of you are normally inseparable. There's absolutely no need to lose your temper."

Josh kicked out at the empty sack that had fluttered to the ground, screaming in frustration as he did so.

"Is there something that you'd like to get off your chest... youngster?"

"Stupid, stupid, stupid, stupid!"

"What's happened to make you so upset?"

Under normal circumstances, Josh wouldn't have had anything to do with the dragon prisoner, not by choice anyway. He hated him, knowing the history that had brought him here, and considered it deeply unfair that he even lived, let alone was being fed and looked after. But circumstances were not normal, and he had no one else to talk to, not even his brother. A mixture of desperation, guilt, worry, anger and fear forced him into the unthinkable.

"I did something... something I don't think he's going to be able to forgive me for... ever!"

Unlucky, surprised at the turnaround of events, and amazed the angry young dragon had deigned to talk to him at all, considered what he'd just heard.

"Family can be a tricky thing. From what I've seen of you both, I can say with absolute certainty that your brother cares for you a great deal. I'd be surprised if he can't forgive you for whatever it is you've done."

"You... you... you don't understand."

"Then explain. My agenda seems to be clear for the rest of the day."

Considering the request carefully, Josh wondered what sort of being could make light of the precarious position they found themselves in, particularly one like this. Was it a strength or a weakness? He didn't know, but on brief reflection, he considered it a weakness. If it was him in that position, there would be no jokes, no friendliness, nothing. But it wasn't him, and at the moment, he had no one else to turn to, not his brother or his... mother.

"I...I...I... betrayed him. I didn't mean to, it just sort of happened."

Unlucky got the feeling there was slightly more to it than that.

"And?"

"My father, he... took my mother hostage to make Man cooperate, threatened her life, told him what he would do if things went badly. It's all my fault, not in my wildest dreams could I have imagined any of this would happen."

So that was it, thought Unlucky. That scum sucking piece of filth of a leader was blackmailing one of his kids through threats of torture and murder to their mother. Suddenly it put his regular beatings into perspective, that's for sure. What to do though, what to do?

Consumed by what he'd done, the younger of the two

siblings dropped to his knees, just out of range of Unlucky, who at the moment had no thought whatsoever about harming the youngster. That hadn't always been the case.

Looking on, the dragon prisoner followed what was left of his conscience and tried to do the right thing.

"I'm sure your brother knows that you would never deliberately do anything to harm either him or your mother."

"I'm not sure he does. The reason he's not here at the moment is because he's off spending time with that creature, off learning how to control his magic, preferring to spend time with him rather than me."

"Perhaps he's choosing to learn about magic while he has the chance. Perhaps he figures that in the long run, he can better help you and your mother out by doing this now, while the opportunity exists. The only way you'll find out for sure is to go and ask him. Why not do that?"

Shaking from the cold and the fright of maybe never seeing, speaking or simply being with his brother again, Josh looked up, frozen tears building up in each of his eyes, desperate for some reassurance that things would be okay.

"Do you think it could be that simple?"

"Honestly... I don't know. It would depend really on exactly how he views your betrayal. Speaking to him would be a start, and you might just be able to get things back on an even keel. Don't expect to repair things straight away though. Forgiveness is different for different beings and in my humble experience, can only fully be offered up over the course of time. My kind often say that time is a great healer, something I can attest to one hundred percent."

A weight taken off his shoulders, Josh staggered to his feet, all the time thinking about the dragon prisoner's wise words.

Unusually for him, he felt compelled to say thank you, and did just that.

"I wish you the best of luck," was Unlucky's reply.

With nothing left to be said, and his chore complete, Josh headed off in the direction of his lessons for the day, contemplating speaking with his brother in an effort to find some sort of common ground and a resolution to their predicament.

Communicating out loud for all to see, well the leader's watchers anyway, and across their telepathic link as well, Marg had started to teach Man the art of firing projectiles and hadn't gotten off to a particularly good start. So much so, that the leader's son had to transform into his prehistoric visage before anything less than complete and utter failure could be contemplated.

Looking majestic in all his ancient, scaled glory, Man found it much easier to direct the ethereal power within him. Commanding the projectiles was fiddly he found, and something about his dragon form made it much more effective and instantaneous.

As Marg produced a dizzying array of floating coloured lights, Man attempted to shoot them down with a range of magical projectiles, including poison, electricity, fire and ice. As you might expect with him being a dragon, the fire was having the most success, destroying all the targets in the quickest time possible. Electricity proved harder to control, and he zapped himself more than once or twice, whilst the poison seemed ungainly and inaccurate, occasionally dissipating before reaching its objective. As for the ice, the less said about that, the better. Difficult and time consuming to produce in the first place, he had yet to hit even one of the targets with a bolt of it so far. The moment the cold left his fingertips, it thudded unceremoniously to the ground, instantly indistinguishable from its surroundings. Pleased with the triumph of the flame, he more than berated himself for his failure with the others. Inside his mind, Marg had much kinder words.

"You're being too hard on yourself. These are difficult

skills to master. To attempt to do so in such a short period of time is almost asking for a miracle. What you've achieved so far, is nothing short of fantastic. If we had three decades to accomplish all of this, we still wouldn't get it done. You have to face the fact that your education will be incomplete to start with and that there's nothing we can do about it."

"I just want to be able to do more," uttered Man in frustration through their invisible link.

"I know youngster, I know. But you're doing brilliantly. You must keep practising. Forget about the ice shards and concentrate on the electricity and poison to see if you can temper those abilities more to your will. You already have control over the fiery flame, but you must add some different arrows to your quill. If you come across something that can barely be hurt by the fire, what will you do?"

"I'm... not sure."

"That's why you need a limited degree of mastery over the poison and the electricity. It won't be perfect, but it will help."

Nodding, Man went on to explain the same misgivings out loud, so that those that were watching could see what was taking place and hopefully stay oblivious to the ongoing deception. Speaking of which, during the course of the training so far today, the elder of the two siblings had started to get the feeling that something, or somethings, were deliberately being withheld and kept out of reach of him. Like an itch you just can't scratch, or something right at the edge of your peripheral vision, apparitions of dark, secretive deadly magic tickled his mind, teased his psyche. Too afraid to ask, wondering if these were all spells he'd be getting to later, he threw all his effort into controlling the wicked bolts of electricity and putrid, luminous green darts of poison. It proved to be the most difficult thing he'd experienced so far.

As the day meandered on, rests were interspersed with

learning, magic zipped and zagged throughout the distant enclave, melting ice, burning holes through rock, incinerating stalactites and stalagmites as well as charging the particles of air throughout the vicinity with all sorts of dangerous supernatural power. On top of learning about projectiles in general, Marg spoke across their undiscovered link about using projectiles as a deception, about sending off a series of projectiles and in what formation, as well as combining different kinds of magic in one overall, almighty attack. It proved to be all-consuming to Man, as well as hugely informative. As the end of the day arrived, and the time for the elder of the two brothers to leave once again, he was disappointed that no mention had been made of the deadly and forbidden magic that he'd just caught a glimpse of in the background earlier. Deciding not to make a scene about it, for obvious reasons, he hoped that with more control over his magic tomorrow, that he might get a chance to acquire such valuable knowledge. Bidding goodbye to the being he now thought of as his friend, he marched off in the direction of some well earned sleep.

Arms bound behind her back, she could barely see through the tiny crystalline structures of the frozen tears that held her eyelids in check. As the cold tortured her body, stabbing here, piercing there, whispered dark words echoed out of the adjacent room. What she heard terrified her to her core. If she could have run, she would. Unfortunately for her, that wasn't an option.

"Report!"

"We've rounded them up as you've asked. They're being kept out of the way in one of the far reaching storage facilities, with guards on hand. Nobody will make their way through, of that we're sure."

"Will anyone notice them missing?"

"Unlikely. The only youngsters that visit the women's

chambers are your sons, and both know better than to do so at the moment."

Although stating only the facts, to some lesser degree or other, the words cut him like a knife. Now though was not the time to be soft, quite the opposite in fact. Now was the time to be bold, adventurous and brave. If things went their way in the coming days, they could all be free, with their powers returned in no time at all. The fact that the remaining women would all have to die was a small price to pay in the scale of things, of that he was sure. What the women thought of that was anybody's guess.

"Are you sure women are the best bet for the process to work?" asked one conspiratorial voice. "What if things go awry? We might need them in the future to procreate once again."

"I think," stated the leader firmly, "that their procreation days are well and truly behind them. For the plan to have the best chance of working, the life force of the females will greatly enhance what we need to do. Their remaining supernatural power should bolster the magic in two or three of us for just long enough if we time things right. After that, it will be a case of using our magic, and those we've taken captive, to do our bidding. If we can capture their leader, the very real threat to him should provide ample incentive for them to not only keep us warm, but help us escape from this freezing hellhole."

In the darkened room directly behind the wall in front of which the despicable men spoke, Man and Josh's mother struggled with all her might upon hearing details of the proposed dirty deed. She wriggled and jiggled, writhed and stretched, using new-found strength at the thought of what they had planned for the women amongst them, her friends and co-workers, beings she regarded and loved. Her struggle, however, was in vain as her sons' father had seen personally to the bonds that held her in place. And although she knew him to be teetering on the edge of insanity, something she'd shielded her boys from, he was nothing if not cautious and thorough. After numerous minutes, and falling down onto her side, she conceded defeat, allowing the cold, monstrous shadows to take her, for once sleep not at all her friend.

Halfway to his pathetic excuse for a private space, a figure garbed in dirty, rotten rags stepped out into the path in front of him from somewhere between a shattered series of crumpled boulders. Just as he'd been taught over the past few days, he raised mental barriers around his mind, and brought forth the spark of supernatural magic from within him that burned bright, so much so that the tips of his fingers glowed in the gloom. As the mysterious figure strolled into what little light existed in and around them, the magic died away, relieved to see, if not quite a friend, certainly not an enemy combatant.

"What do you want?" Man asked harshly, wanting nothing more than to get back and lose himself in some well deserved sleep.

It didn't look as though it was going to be that easy.

"We... we... we... need to talk," stuttered his brother, all the time keeping his voice friendly and low.

"There's nothing else to talk about. You've chosen which side you're on by betraying your mother and brother. How you could do such a thing is totally and utterly beyond me."

Standing facing each other by now, Man sidestepped right in an effort to get past. Quicker than he would have thought possible, his sibling blocked his path, determined to have this out. Hands on hips, Man just stood and glared, something nobody wanted to be on the end of, least of all Josh.

"You... you... you seemed so convinced not to help. I didn't want to get you in trouble with Father, I just... I...

just thought that if he knew how you felt, then he could have a chat, make you see the bigger picture. I had no idea he would do that to Mother, you have to believe me Man, you just have to."

He had to do nothing of the sort, that much was for sure. But standing there, watching his traitor of a brother try and justify his actions, forced his temper to rise, really got his goat, and so without hesitation, he responded.

"You've got a bloody cheek seeking me out, trying to apologise for your treachery," he spat, jabbing his index finger deep into the middle of his sibling's chest.

So taken aback by this was Josh, that he stumbled back on his heels, nearly slipping on the ice and falling flat on his arse. Blind luck stopped this from happening.

"I... I... I... I never meant for that to happen. I was just worried... for you, and for Mother and for..."

"Worried for yourself more like," growled Man, his temper hanging by a thread. "You didn't give a damn about either of us. You just thought you'd use it as a way to get in with Father."

"No... no... no," babbled Josh. "That's not it, that's not it at all."

"I don't believe you, and neither does Mother, particularly not in her current predicament. Why don't you run on back to whatever little hole you've crawled out of, and wait for some faint semblance of praise from your father. After all, that's what you've been hoping for isn't it?"

Pointing and shaking demonstrably, Josh stood in front of one of the only two beings he loved on the entire planet, eyes wide, mouth snarled, anger at not being listened to and instantly forgiven, rising with every moment that passed.

"I tried," he shouted, not caring now who heard. "All I wanted to do was leave this place. Is that so bad? But you... you decide in your great wisdom that your precious morals are more important, more important than everyone here leaving this icy prison. Well... bully for you, I hope your morality brings you great comfort when you're still trapped her fifty years from now."

Man reached out, and in a blur, grabbed his brother by the rags around his neck, pulling him forward, now close enough to feel his freezing breath wash across his face.

"What's the point of living if we can't lead a decent life? Treachery, betrayal, deception... and that's just amongst his own kind. Exactly what kind of leader is our father? Someone you look up to, someone you admire and want to follow in his footsteps? Pathetic! I'd rather be trapped in here knowing that I'm a decent, honest and kind being, just as my mother raised me, than have anything to do with that slimy piece of filth. He's only my father in name... that's all. I want nothing to do with him, his policies or his plans. You forget what he's already done, what our mother's already endured, up until now. And then you do this... betray the both of us, all for what? You're a joke and one that I want nothing to do with. You had your chance to choose, and I'll tell you now, you've made an almighty mistake. So get lost," Man cried, throwing his brother back a full five metres, "and don't come near me again. If you do, you won't walk away in one piece."

Barely containing the rage threatening to erupt out of him, the elder of the two stormed off in the direction of his tiny little space, determined to ignore and not touch the flickering and sparking magic that threatened to consume him. Ignoring its touch and desire to be used, a few minutes later he laid down his head and as a cacophony of emotions assaulted his very being, drifted off to sleep.

During what would be regarded as the early hours of the morning, and with most of the community asleep, the leader, his second in command and a couple of the other thugs that they could trust, silently made their way from one side of the compound to the other, arriving half an hour or so later, at a heavily guarded entrance that few knew about.

"Are they all in there?" asked the leader to the head guard.

"They are."

"Do they know what's going on?"

"No. They're only aware of what's happened to them, not what's in store."

"Good. It'll all be over in an hour or so. Make sure no one comes anywhere near here."

Clasping his comrade tightly on the shoulder, recognising the look of uncertainty in his eyes, the leader spoke firmly and surely, for all those around to hear.

"We're so close, it's almost possible to touch it... escape I mean. But we can't give in now. We have to be strong and stick to the plan. Of course it's risky and not ideal, as well as being repugnant, but if it pays off, and I truly believe in my heart of hearts that it will, then it'll have been worth it. Their sacrifices won't have been in vain, and will lead to not only a better life for all of us, but a foundation on which to build the renewal of the planet. The much bigger picture here, is that we can shape the face of the earth, but first of all we have to make sacrifices, much as we don't want to. What happens here today shall be remembered forever. Nobody will be forgotten, on that you all have my word."

In total and utter silence, each one of the men there bowed their heads in subjugation, knowing that their leader was right, ashamed that they'd doubted him at all, and infused with righteous belief in what they were doing. Dark, desperate deeds, in their minds at least, had become totally and utterly justified. It was time.

Accompanied by his second in command, and two of his men chosen not only for their loyalty, but because of the strength of the power they contained in their natural personas, the leader strolled into the storage facility, all too focused on the job at hand. It had to be done for the greater good, that was what continued to drive him on.

Cowered against the furthest icy wall, clad in filthy strips of material, the remaining seventeen women of the penal colony, with the exception of Man and Josh's mother, looked a state. Having long since foregone their sleek, sensual, prehistoric figures due to the harsh temperatures, the females did little justice to their true forms, or at least that's what the leader's first thought was. Most beings in this situation would at least have felt some pity or remorse for what they were about to do. Not him though.

"Bring me the first one," he ordered brutally, not even a hint of emotion resonating in his voice.

Two of his men picked one of the females at random, and dragging her by the hair, pulled her over to their leader, kicking and screaming, throwing her to the floor at his feet.

"Hold her down," he commanded, as the others watched on.

They did as they were told, all the time ignoring the defenceless woman's screaming and struggles.

Placing his open palm on her forehead, the leader closed his eyes and within his mind, recounted ancient, forbidden magic, wishing for it to be over. Unfortunately for him, it had yet to begin.

Cool, yellow light enveloped the tips of his fingers and the female's forehead. Immediately her thrashing about stopped, her body becoming quiet and compliant. The whimpering from the others stopped. Ice cold silence encompassed everything.

Locked away in a shadowy, black cage, his thoughts surrounded her magic, marvelling at its beauty, enthralled by its power. Tailing off, a straggling strand of light twisted and turned, this way and that, disappearing off somewhere deep inside her body. No doubt the binding to her life force, he supposed, no longer interested, only caring about what he could take and how much effort it would cost him. Turning in an instant, a cool, calculated rage consumed him. Using his mind as a sledgehammer, he struck the first blow against the cage, pleasure rushing through him as huge, zigzagging cracks cut across its frame, weakening its structure immensely. Through tiny little openings, supernatural power shone out, the colours looking like facets of a diamond. One more blow should do it, he knew, that's how close he was. Aware of the consequences of his actions, he battered the remaining defences with everything he had. An explosion without sound was his stark reward, a superheated ball of energy infusing his very essence, inundating his whole self, a power that he hadn't felt in many, many decades unlocking familiar sensations and abilities. An ecstasy the likes of which he'd never known consumed every atom of his being, the prehistoric monster hidden deep within him for so long roared at being finally awoken. Around him the earth trembled, ice peeled from the walls, stalactites and stalagmites crumbled into nothingness, and rocks tumbled from the ceiling. For all intents and purposes, it was an announcement, not only to those around him, but to the world and its denizens. Something from far in the past had come home, seeking to right a wrong and return to what it considered its rightful place. Evil rejoiced momentarily. It wouldn't be long now, it really wouldn't.

Right in front of their eyes, the scared and wretched female form being held down by two of the vicious thugs, glowed fleetingly, before the skin on the outside started to contract. As a collective intake of breath ricocheted around the enclosure, the by now withered skin melted into nothingness, leaving a bare, solitary skeleton stuck to the icy floor. It was enough to start a riot. The remaining women prisoners went mad, some trying to evade the guards and run away, others risking life and limb by fighting hand to hand with them. After approximately ten seconds, wicked, dark blue magic surged forth from their leader's hands, knocking the women to the floor, stunning and paralysing them all. One by one, the essence of their lives were given over to the leader, his second in command, and the two others with them. Seven of the women's lives were claimed by the leader, increasing his supernatural power exponentially, four for the second in command with both of the thugs taking three lives each, revelling in the dark deeds that had returned ethereal power which they thought of as rightfully theirs, and had on numerous occasions wondered if they'd ever experience again. So here they were, a fighting force of four, but four of the most powerful, most despicable, beings ever to stalk the earth. If those across the planet had known what had just occurred, most would have cowered in fear. As it was, this was played out in one of the most desolate, remote and unlikely places, with only a handful of individuals knowing what had gone on. Secrecy would play its part, and if things worked out, then life forms across the world needed to watch out. One thing was for certain... they'd be coming for you.

Before leaving the freezing room full of tattered rags and skeletons, the leader gave out orders. One of the two men with their powers returned, was ordered to take up a position in the cavern with the dragon prisoner by the stream and use the magic that he'd just regained to watch out for any approaching parties of beings... in particular, nagas. The leader explained that he had a hunch that the naga king and his lackeys wouldn't be too far out by now. With a bit of notice, it might be possible to arrange an appropriate greeting for them. Wouldn't that be nice?! The other was to stand guard over the naga Marg's private room, and cloak it with a very specific, undetectable magic, one that should stop any telepathic messages getting in or out. It wouldn't do to have Marg and the naga king contacting each other, especially given the leader's concerns about what the naga and Man were up to. Cutting off all surreptitious telepathic contact seemed like the right thing to do.

Atop the block of ice that he slept upon, Man was briefly awoken, sure that he'd heard something... a rock slide maybe, or ice or snow falling from high up on the walls. But as quickly as it had come, it disappeared, and with no one else rushing to either help or see what had happened, he figured it must have been part of his dreams, which of late had become more nightmarish than anything else. Quickly he dozed back off.

At his remote enclave, Marg was abruptly startled awake, not so much by the sound of rocks and ice moving, but more like a prickling sensation of darkness piercing his scales all over. Never before had he felt such malevolence or maliciousness. A chill, not from the temperature or the frozen water all around him, crept up from his tail, gorging itself on his innards, attempting to consume his very soul. Something, somewhere close by, was very, very wrong, he knew.

Having overslept, unusually, Man finally turned up to find his naga cohort looking frazzled and agitated. Settling down on the floor next to him, through their shared telepathic bond, the young boy dragon asked what was wrong.

"You didn't feel it last night?"

"No... at least I don't think so. I woke up startled at one point, but I didn't think too much of it."

"I bet that was it," declared Marg. "Almost certainly the magic inside you giving you a subtle hint."

"A hint as to what?"

"Of that my young friend, I can't be sure. But something significant happened last night, of that much I am certain. We should continue with our lessons, with great haste. I envisage having to use what you've learnt, very shortly."

And so they did, continuing with their discussions about projectiles, Marg eluding to the theory of throwing fireballs, something that was far from his specialities given how much nagas dislike anything hot or fiery, all the time appearing outwardly calm and relaxed, inside feeling anything but.

Another twenty four hours passed without incident, before the leader's man at the cavern with the stream reported that he needed to see him as a matter of urgency, through the secretive telepathic link that they'd established after regaining their magical dragon powers. In only a matter of minutes the leader arrived, his speed bolstered by the supernatural power that had always been his.

Tucking themselves away out of sight of the bound and restrained dragon prisoner, the chief asked the question that had been on his mind since the very first message.

"Report!"

"They're out there, I'm sure of it."

"Really?"

"I've had contact a few times now. It's almost as if they swim in and out of range. If I had to guess, I'd say they're a few hours out, but moving in this general direction."

"Can you let me experience it for myself?"

"Sure," whispered his man, opening up his telepathic link fully with the leader, whilst at the same time reaching out to the furthest extent with all the magic he had. Both waited patiently, their heartbeats slowed, their breathing quiet but regular, anticipating what was to come.

There... there... again! He could see it through his mind's eye now, contacts, large intelligent ones at that, and more than a few, all heading slowly this way from a point far upstream. It could be no one else. Slapping his underling on the shoulder for good measure, and with a smile on his face, he sprinted off at pace, using his power to keep him upright and out of danger, eager to get back to his room. As he dashed past the restrained dragon, his face contorted into a snarl of defiance, something the prisoner recognised for what it was. The enemy had their magic back, he thought, and so the world was in a whole host of trouble. Inside, Unlucky quaked at what he'd just seen. Bad enough the display of anger and displeasure towards him, indicating that yet another beating was imminent, but the speed with which he ran could only mean one thing, and that terrified him more than repeated torture, or even dying in this unforgiving hellhole. Things had changed, and he had no idea how or even why. This was bad... very, very bad.

After dishing out the orders, he knew now that there was simply no turning back. Too much had been achieved, too much had been sacrificed. It was now or never. Do or die. And so resigned to everything so long in the making, he accepted this period of relative calm before the storm, and headed off to see his son and their current naga guest, all the while wondering who had been teaching who.

From out of nowhere, Man's father came storming through the entrance, a deep seated look of satisfaction etched across his face. Instinctively, and without any kind of give-away, both naga and student erected their respective mental barriers, determined not to get caught off guard, even though in this environment there should be little or no threat.

"How goes the training?" the leader asked, taking in everything around him.

"We progress well, if not a little slowly," answered Marg, a slight hiss in the background of his voice, the only giveaway that he wasn't human. "Crossing the magical boundaries of naga and dragon are not only complicated but exhausting as well. But the youngster shows spirit and guile, something any good sorcerer should possess in spades."

"Indeed, indeed."

Having been lured into a false sense of security, it was then that the sucker punch arrived, truly out of nowhere.

"Why don't you tell me what you've really been doing?" demanded the leader, a sickly, smug grin crawling across his face.

In both of their minds, a collective 'uh oh,' rang out like a village church bell late at night.

"I'm not sure what you mean," replied the naga, sounding as sincere as possible.

"Oh don't be coy. I know all about your schemes and plans. Do you think me stupid?"

Every molecule of Man's body was screaming out in terror, transfixed at how badly this had gone and how quickly it had happened. From nothing to something in less than a heartbeat, something that could be their undoing unless he acted fast.

"Father..."

A backhanded slap with all the ferocity and power of a fighter jet caught Man just beneath the jaw, sending him sprawling across the open space, smashing clumsily into the rocky wall some twenty or so metres away, sliding comically down onto the slippery floor as he did so. Looking on in disbelief, if Marg still had any doubts about his friend's intentions, they'd all been washed away now. As the leader and the naga faced off, magic hummed across the air, igniting the molecules between them, almost alive, with a will of its own. It had been more decades than he could recall since he'd last fought with the supernatural power that was his. Only now did he realise just how much he'd missed it, only now did he truly relish the prospect of battle. As blood seeped through Man's lips and onto the brilliant, icy white of the floor beneath him, he struggled to get to his feet, struggled to make the difference he knew he had to.

"I don't want to fight you," Marg told the leader, "but if I have to I will. Defeat is all you've got to look forward to."

Over the course of his time there as a guest, or not, so to speak, the naga, a keen observer of everything, had taken an interest in all that he had seen. And although recognising that their leader, standing before him now, had somehow regained a fraction of his magical ability, Marg really didn't see it as any sort of threat. He knew that he was stronger, more quick witted, better suited to the environment and able to wield everything he had at a moment's notice. Of one thing he was absolutely certain, that he would be the outright winner in a fight, and would go on and take out every being here if need be. Wrong wouldn't necessarily be the right word to describe the naga's thinking, after all, it was only his opinion, but he was far off the mark, failing to recognise the will, and more importantly, the evil intent behind his opponent's power. If he had, then he would have been not only fearful for his life, but for that of his new found friend as well.

"I suppose you think you're clever with your secret telepathic link and your twisted plots and plans," the leader sneered.

"It was never my intention to cause any harm. I just want to get back to my kin, return to the sea and leave all this behind me. Set me free, and we can forget any of this ever happened."

It was exactly at that point that Marg felt the first familiar touch, some way off in the distance. A coiled surge of fear and panic started to unravel within him, recognising not only his monarch, but his companions as well. Metres away, the leader's sickly grin spread out across his wicked face.

"Are they getting closer by any chance?" he quipped.

For Marg, it was the last straw. There was no way in hell he was leading the king of his kind into any sort of trap, something this was clearly designed to be. Without hesitation, and with his heart as cold as the immediate surroundings, he called forth his ancient magic, and set about destroying these fools.

There was, however, only one problem, one that he was unable to envisage, one that if he'd recognised it, would have caused him to flee rather than fight. You see the being he found himself faced off against, the leader of this rag tag community of would be dragons, although not having access to all his supernatural powers, and looking pretty pitiful in magical terms, had been, in his day, one of the most powerful and dangerous beings to ever have walked the earth. Even after many, many decades locked up in an icy prison like this, you simply don't lose the danger, the arrogance or the attitude. What Man's father currently lacked in ethereal ability, he more than made up for with his sense of self-importance, superior belief and his willingness to do absolutely anything for his cause, no matter how despicable and depraved. In short, he would stop at nothing to get his way, something the misinformed naga was about to find out.

Too caught up in his current predicament to warn his monarch, knowing that he would as soon as he could, Marg allowed the magic to consume him and in his mind started to utter the words that would bring the dragon leader to his knees, quite literally. But before his power could obey that command, his mental defences were torn asunder, thrown to the wind, scattered across time, never to be seen again.

A serpent-like hissing howl filled the chamber as the imposing naga collapsed to the floor with a deafening THUD, causing ice to crack and the rocky walls to shake. Having staggered to the floor, Man looked on in disbelief at what had just happened, two thoughts alone dominating his mind.

How the hell had his dad just taken down Marg, and what did this mean for him?

Elsewhere in the prison, Josh had been asked to accompany three of his father's men in the direction of the naga guest's sanctuary. Unsure of what was going on, and caught off guard, he could do nothing but comply.

With nothing but the gurgling of the stream for company, Unlucky fought off the cold in his usual way, sorting out memories of happier times from long in the past, allowing his mind to wander, taking him away to anywhere but here. Unfortunately, that only lasted so long before reality returned, usually with a bump. Opening his eyes, his body shivering uncontrollably, the first thing he noticed was the bloodthirsty looking human shape, still on the lookout over by the stream. 'Odd,' was what he'd thought when he'd arrived the previous day, but now it was just downright strange. That combined with the fact that their leader seemed to have some semblance of his magic back, gave him grave cause for concern. As his stomach rumbled from not having been fed, he wondered where the elder of the two brothers who normally brought him food was, and just what was going on as a whole. Were they waiting for someone to arrive? Could they have actually got a message out? Was his time here about to come to a crushing end? Those were all questions that played on his mind as he courageously battled the cold and tried to stave off unconsciousness.

Clawing at the floor with his fingernails, forked tongue hissing like an out of control steam train, his tail twitching and writhing, Marg's mind was not his own, his mental defences now nonexistent thanks to the furious and outrageous attack by the leader, evil intent combined with ancient dragon magic and know-how, no match for a naive young naga.

Sifting through the alien landscape of another being's mind was both pleasurable and exotic, the leader found. Satisfaction at smothering his enemy's mental defences almost instantly caused him great delight as he searched scattered alien thoughts. Spells, hexes, recipes for magical artefacts, as well as detailed maps of this whole region, flooded every part of him, his eidetic memory taking in every last piece of information. Almost overwhelmed, he forced himself to continue, take every last scrap, knowing that this might be his one chance, concern about the effect he was having on the naga's mind nowhere to be seen.

Mental defences intact and erect, Man unsteadily stood, appalled at what was happening to his new found friend, wondering whether or not to launch an all-out attack on his father, who for now, at least, seemed to be ignoring him.

Caught up in another's psyche was proving to be much better than he could ever remember. Of course he'd done this before, hundreds of times in fact, taking what he wanted whether his enemy liked it or not, subjugating others to his will, even on occasion taking lives in this fashion. It wasn't the easiest way to do that, but there was something about it that he found quite refreshing, at least that's what his memories were telling him. In the past though, he'd only ever used it against dragons... members of his own race, intellects familiar, filled with thoughts, ideas and secrets that all made sense to him. Now though... wow, this was something else altogether. Unfamiliar script wove in and out of his consciousness, accompanied by strange thoughts, details about magical restraints and foreign spells. It was both a delight and a torment being there. If he'd understood it all, it would have been great. Because he couldn't, he quickly became frustrated, rushing his rummaging around, hastily damaging everything in his way in the search for the truth. THERE! In his rush, he almost missed it... almost. Only moments ago, an attempted contact from outside of this prison... it must be them, surely it must be them. Caught up in the mind of another, answers coming thick and fast, momentarily the outside world failed to exist for him, all sense of danger totally ignored.

Watching Marg's excruciating agony and his father's stony delight, Man could take no more, and so setting his morality free and feeding off the disgust he felt at what was going on, he dipped into his well of magic and, unleashing the most powerful of the spells that he'd learnt during the previous day's teachings, he used all his will to send out a hail of supernatural projectiles, aiming them squarely at his father's exposed back.

In less than the blink of an eye, the magic passed between them. The youngster had learnt well, applying all his considerable will behind it, remaining fully focused despite the situation. Unfortunately though, he'd made one costly mistake. He'd chosen to use fire as his primary method, and whilst this was his strongest form of offence, he should have taken into consideration that he was taking on a dragon, alright, one in its human guise, but nevertheless, still a dragon, and dragons everywhere, no matter what their persona, still have an affinity with and natural defences against... FIRE!

Wide-eyed at having just discovered some of the most deadly, dark, vile and evil magic he'd ever seen, abruptly alarm bells rang out deep inside his head. Attempting to look over his shoulder in the direction of his son, it was then that the projectiles slammed into his exposed back, drilling holes into his skin, scorching his organs, setting alight the tattered rags that he wore.

"Aaaaarrrggghhhhhh!" he screamed, dropping to his knees, waves of agonising pain piercing every nerve ending inside him.

If Man weren't so naive, and had experienced even the most basic battle training, he would have known to finish off a difficult, cunning and deadly opponent while he had the chance. But that knowledge did not reside inside him, that and the fact that it was his father suffering, was enough to take his eye off the ball so to speak. And so he just stood and watched his father twist and writhe in misery, flames burning his skin, madness and anger spilling over, his shrieks of pain reverberating around the cavern.

Intruder instantly gone from his mind, Marg collapsed to the ground, soaking up the cold, mind in tatters, unable to form any coherent thought at all. Far away, a cool, calculating magic locked onto his naga essence and began tracking its way to him. The king's cohorts had found what they were looking for, and were now headed this way. The leader's plan was coming together nicely, with the exception of just one thing.

Roaring like a lion having just been stung on the trumpet, Man's father went absolutely ballistic, rising to his feet, shaking off the remnants of what passed for his clothing, sending brightly glowing, brilliant orange embers scattering into the air.

Instantly Man took two steps back, as the crazed form of his burning dad whirled around furiously, yelling and screaming, kicking, stamping and waving his arms angrily, enraged and infuriated, searching for some kind of target. Only at that very moment, did the elder of the two brothers realise the trouble he was in. Cursing very loudly in his mind, and willing his friend the naga to get up and join the fight, Man readied his defences, exactly as he'd been taught, and prepared for the onslaught that he knew, without doubt, would be coming his way.

Pain and fury punctured every nerve, every vein, every blood vessel, every major organ, decimating his will, destroying his desire to live. All he wanted was to be rid of it, for things to be at an end. Instinctively he tried to climb to his feet, his body moving of its own accord, the pain taking it this way and that, arms whirring like drunken windmills. But he failed miserably. From out of nowhere, and somewhere deep inside the despicable depths that made up his character, a rising, unforgiving voice shouted over the maelstrom of charred bone and burning tissue,

"GET UP! DO IT NOW!"

Without delay, he rose to his feet, all the time fighting the blistering agony that had enveloped the whole of his body.

"FIGHT BACK! IT'S WHAT YOU DO!"

Those words caused him to remember... fighting back, anyway.

Twirling around, a ballet dancer ablaze, something caught his attention through the fire, flame and tortuous haze... his SON! Standing there, smoke and ethereal tendrils of flame from the magic he'd dispensed still hanging in the air directly above his fingertips, looking terrified and afraid.

"AS WELL HE SHOULD!" screamed the voice, urging on its owner to much darker deeds.

As if it was the most natural thing in the world, the leader thrust out his arm, opened out his smouldering fingers and willed his magic to work. It did, and to great effect.

Brightly coloured dark blue and purple crisscrossing lines of flickering, zigzagging convulsive electricity lit up the cavern, from the reflections on the smooth surfaces all around, adding to the terror and anticipation Man felt in no small way. Before the first sign of current had even got near him, he was absolutely petrified, unable to move even a muscle. An instant later, the full force of the supernatural onslaught devoured his body in the most painful of embraces, setting his teeth on fire, making his eyeballs burn, pricking his skin with a billion razor sharp needles, splintering his finger and toenails, tearing at his genitals. As the confusion, pain, rip-roaring agony and fright gripped him, instantly he wished for unconsciousness to take him, or even to die. Unfortunately, he wasn't nearly that lucky. Tongue charred like the worst case of burnt toast, tiny little bolts of electricity continued to zip around inside his mouth, glancing off teeth, the roof of his mouth and then his charred, limp tongue. It was all encompassing, and more importantly, a telling lesson.

As his son struggled, the leader, although still in dire straits, gained the upper hand. That is until a long, scaled appendage whistled across the floor, knocking him off his feet, sending him clattering to the frosty ground, a loud CRACK accompanied by screech of pain.

Through the crazed agony and the mind-bending pain that gripped his body, Man could vaguely make out words somewhere off in the distance.

"You must finish him off now, while he's vulnerable. If you don't, then we're all doomed."

His first thought was that he didn't understand either the meaning, or who the words belonged to. As the moments passed his thought process began to clear despite the pain. A split second later and he had it. Marg! The words belonged to his friend, lying face down on the floor, his giant tail having just brushed away his father's legs. He had to act, and now.

Scared beyond belief, not only at the thought of taking a life for the very first time, but of his father, confusion and indecision ate away at him from the inside, preventing him from taking immediate action. If it hadn't, and he'd just got on with the job, he might have saved them all. As it stood, doom was about to come knocking.

As his father once again crawled to his knees, his brother, and then mother, were thrust through the entrance to the enclave by a group of his father's men. Shaking uncontrollably from the electricity still zipping around his system, Man took one uncertain step in their direction, before a harsh voice stopped him in his tracks.

"STOP!" bellowed his father.

Unsurprisingly, he did as he was told, his only current concern, the fate of his mother.

"If he takes one more step towards either of them, or looks to ignite his magic as a threat... kill her," commanded his father to one of the thugs. Immediately the dragon in human form pulled a sharp, scorched piece of metal from about his body, and pulling the woman's hair back, held it tightly against her throat.

"NO!" screamed her eldest son, desperate to stop anything bad from happening to her.

"I TOLD YOU WHAT WOULD HAPPEN SHOULD YOU DEFY ME!" screamed the leader. "YOU'LL BE SORRY YOU'VE GONE AGAINST ME!"

"No... no... no I'll do anything you want, please... just don't hurt her."

"ANYTHING?"

"Yes... yes... yes anything. I promise."

Strolling casually across the chamber towards the source of the attack that had caused him so much pain, the leader finally had the chance to cast a series of healing mantras, quelling the flames, quenching his burning bones, healing the damaged tissue and replacing lost blood. Relief washed over him as he vanquished the agony, well... most of it anyway. Standing directly in front of his cowed son, one thought and one thought only raced around inside his head. Most beings might have been able to resist. Not this one.

In a blur, his leg kicked out, his foot effortlessly smashing through the kneecap of his son, a huge explosion of breaking bone echoing around the chamber, causing Josh and his mother to cry out and wince at the same time. Man hit the floor hard, brutal waves of extraordinary pain coursing up his leg, inundating him with feelings the likes of which he'd never known. Much more on top of things, the leader crouched down next to his felled son, and placed his hand on the boy's broken knee. To a man and a woman, everyone there watching figured that after teaching the youngster a lesson, his father would now offer up some much needed supernatural healing. Given the leader's inherently dark nature, what happened next really shouldn't have come as a surprise. Using something from the naga's mind he'd only moments ago invaded against its will, a spell that translated roughly as 'sonic crusher', the leader placed his fingertips into the gaping knee wound that had shards of bone sticking out, and let rip with all the willpower he possessed. If the onlookers had considered anything that had gone on previously to be painful, this took things up a notch or ten. Instantly Man screamed, or at least tried to with the charred tongue that no longer served its purpose. Strange, angry, sucking noises were all that came out as he rolled around in outstanding agony. As he finished, fully aware that his son, whenever now in that shape would carry more than a little limp, he leaned in close and whispered,

"That's for you to remember me by. Don't ever go up against me again."

Through the confusion and angst of it all, Man healed himself as best he could, melting away at least most of the pain, but not when it came to his knee. Something about that felt wrong, and more permanent than anything else. A rising tide of anger nipping at his heels, he fought back an urge to act, knowing that his mother was still in danger. As he did so though, a singular thought occupied his mind. If she could be made safe... what then? Aware that Josh was within an arm's length of his mother's throat, and could through a combination of surprise and overwhelming strength negate the threat quite quickly, if that were the case, it would give him enough time to transform into his prehistoric natural form, and finish things off once and for all. Nobody would be able to stop them. As well, if he communicated his plan to Marg, the naga just might be able to help them, even in his injured state.

From his position on the floor, Man grabbed hold of his magic, and using all his will, forced himself inside his brother's mind. When it was done, and he was sure no one could tell what was going on, least of all his father, he spoke in a hushed whisper, so as not to surprise Josh.

"Brother, can you hear me? Don't speak out loud... I'm inside your mind."

"Man?"

"That's right."

"What's going on? Why are you here?"

"I need your help to keep Mother safe."

"W... w... what do you want me to do?"

"If you can get that weapon away from her throat, I'll do the rest."

"How on earth are you going to do that? No offence, but you don't look like you're in a position to do anything."

"I'm going to change back into my dragon form. They won't stand a chance once that's happened."

"Do you really think it will work?"

"I think it's the best chance there is. Do you really want to do nothing and see how this all plays out? I guarantee he's going to kill Mother, no matter what we do now, you can just see it in his eyes."

Inside Josh's head, he agreed wholeheartedly.

"So will you help?"

"Yes," decided his brother.

"I'm going to see if our naga friend there can create some sort of distraction. Wait for my signal."

And with that, their communication was lost, leaving Josh standing next to his mother, more than a little gobsmacked at what had just happened.

Outstretched on the icy hard ground, brain scrambled, barely able to put a coherent thought together, Marg was an absolute mess. That still didn't stop him from trying to rally against it all. If nothing else, nagas were stubborn and at times possessed a single minded will like no other being on the planet. And with a clear and present threat to his monarch which felt very much like his fault, he attempted to do all that he could in an effort to rectify the situation.

"Marg, it's me... Man," floated a soft velvety voice across his psyche.

Garbled thoughts tumbled around his mind, singular words trying to capture his attention.

'Trap, friend, help, betray, coming, here, now, danger, sorry.' It was almost impossible to separate them all.

Ignoring his friend's muddled mind, the elder of the two brothers continued.

"I need you to create a distraction. Can you help?"

Words whistled around between the two of them, the naga unable to express his opinion clearly.

'Tragedy, save, fight, death blame, escape, foreboding, rescue, pain, wickedness, violence, destruction, lies, manipulation, kin, truth, scapegoat.'

It was painful to hear across the link, and broke Man's heart, but still he pushed on.

"MARG!" he shouted over the sound of the words, drifting along on the wind between them. "I need your help. Please can you create some kind of distraction? I think it just might be enough to save us all."

Sanity returned, albeit briefly.

"I'll do what I can... friend."

And with that, silence encompassed their link.

Man took a breath, readied himself to unlock the strands of DNA that would affect the change and prepared to give his brother the signal. If this didn't work, quite literally they were all dead.

"In a movement so quick, it was just one long continuous blur, the naga strewn out on the floor whipped its snake-like body around and leapt up and across towards the leader, its razor sharp teeth clamping down on the bottom part of his leg, eliciting the mother of all screams as it did so.

Man didn't even need to tell his brother to react, he was already on it. Coiled like a spring, Josh jumped his attacker, forcing his arm between the sharpened shiv and his mother's throat, sickly red blood spurting everywhere as the blade sliced open his frozen skin.

Watching with pride at his brother's selfless act, Man

sent the command, closed his eyes and as the feeling gripped every part of his body, prepared for action, welcoming a return to what he considered his natural form.

Caught off guard, the leader's first reaction was to kick his leg out in an effort to shake free of the naga's frenzied attack. With teeth like that, and a vice-like grip, needless to say it didn't work. Only focusing on this one thing, with the lethal threat taking up all his concentration, he was blissfully unaware of everything playing out around him.

Watching her son's arm only a few centimetres from her face, sliced open like a soft, rare fruit, by one of their father's thuggish brutes raised her hackles more than a little. So in a fit of fury, the protective side of her came to the fore, and in the blink of an eye, she leant forward and tore a huge chunk of flesh off the attacker's hand with her teeth, immediately spitting it out, off to one side. Crying out in pain at the savage attack, instinctively their opponent dropped his weapon. Seizing his chance, Josh whirled around, and with all the speed and ferocity that he could muster, slammed his elbow into his enemy's face, his reward, a satisfying CRACK that sent the threat plummeting to the ground. Only then did they both notice the second guard, all but upon them, waving around another homemade shiv. Defenceless, both backed away, but it was far too late for that. Instantly, he dived forward, intent on making them pay.

Words, thoughts, memories drifted in and out of one another, forcing him to relive tragedy, hope, despair and happiness in all but a moment. Clinging onto what he thought of as reality, he kept his jaws clamped tight around the leg of what he knew to be his enemy, and with all his might, used his strong body to wriggle and sway, tossing the leader of this dark and deadly place around like a rag doll in the air. This one thought, 'I MUST keep the leader busy, because my friend is in trouble,' pierced the veil of his mind, keeping him on the straight and narrow. How long it would last was anybody's guess.

As the razor sharp blade cut through the air towards them, it seemed as though both of their lives were about to end abruptly, mother and son going out in a blaze of glory, both attempting to wrong a right, both terrified beyond belief. But as the blade got within a hairsbreadth of the mother's throat, suddenly the attacker's momentum died, as two humungous, prehistoric jaws crunched together, encasing the attacker's whole body, sending bone, muscle and blood pelting into the walls and floor all around them. With one shake of his giant, prehistoric, light blue head, Man tossed what remained of the cadaver halfway across the room, and with a satisfying roar, knowing that his mother and brother were safe, stomped off towards his besieged father, limping ever so slightly as he did so.

Disappointed beyond belief at both the pain from his leg and everything relating to their current situation, the leader vowed to correct this instantly. Aware that he wasn't going to be able to open the naga's jaws and free his leg, of course nothing could be that simple, he decided instead to try a workaround. And so sliding his right hand into the slightest of gaps between the beast's teeth, he pushed down as far as he could with his arm, whilst at the same time conjuring up as much of his magic as he dared. Deciding in an instant on fire, knowing that almost certainly this would be the monster's Achilles heel, he unleashed a barrage of flame and heat directly down the fiend's throat.

A bone chilling screech was the leader's reward for a job well done, that and the immediate release of his leg, for which he was hugely grateful.

Snake-like skull crashing to the ground with a THUD, the game was nearly up for Marg. Mirroring his friend with a hugely charred forked tongue, the inside of his mouth very much resembled a pizza oven, without of course the Italian delicacies. Barely able to take a breath, what he did manage to inhale was mostly smoke, which only added to his already addled brain. Coughing, choking and wheezing, through the mire of his mind he searched for reality, hoping to do his friend one last favour.

Turning on a dime, washing away the pain from the needle sharp teeth marks in his leg with just a touch of ethereal power, he was then confronted by a huge prehistoric shape towering over him... his SON! Pleased at noticing the limp he still had, despite his change in shape, the leader took a few furtive steps back, considering his position and predicament. Ideally he needed his son, with all his new found powers and that intimidating dragon shape, to be on his side. What he could really do without, was going head to head with him here and now, not only because of what was to come, but because he really couldn't be sure of winning, not without all of his power and the ability to take his natural form. Working on the puzzle, he tried to buy himself some time.

"Take a little time to think about what you're doing, son," he suggested calmly to the gigantic ancient shape hovering over him.

Man thought about it for a split second, but the vision of Marg's tortured body writhing around in the background made him angry, more so than he could ever remember being, that and the fact that his father had tried to have his mother killed mere moments ago.

"NO!" he bellowed in a low, gruff voice, something so different from that of his human guise.

"What I've done, I've done for all of us, so that we can break free, and take our rightful place in the world again. Harsh choices had to be made, and there was no one else to do it. Don't think I've taken those decisions lightly... I haven't. They've tortured my conscience, and given me many a sleepless night."

"Conscience?" scoffed Man, his huge dinosaur-like head weaving this way and that, tiny sniffles of flame skirting his nostrils as he did so. "You don't have a conscience, in fact I'm surprised you even know what the word means. As for sleepless nights, I think the only thing that gives you sleepless nights is the fact that you aren't free yet. I think you'd gladly sacrifice every last one of us here for your freedom, in a heartbeat."

It was almost as if the young boy was a mind reader, thought his father, rather perturbed. And he was much more insightful and intelligent than he'd ever given him credit for. This was so not going the way he'd planned it. He needed an opportunity, and he needed one now.

Hugging each other tight, mother and son sheltered behind the massive, reassuring shadow of Man, an overwhelming sense of joy gripping them both at being temporarily safe, and having the person that they loved between them and their psychotic leader. Neither wanted to ever leave the comfort of the other two, now more so than ever, with both wishing the huge dragon in front of them all the luck in the world with the choice he faced about what to do next. In reality they knew a choice hardly existed, and that this was only going to go one way. In the end, he'd do what was right, they both knew, freeing not only them, but the rest of the community from a crazed and cruel leader. Not wanting to watch exactly how this played out, they knew that for Man's sake they just had to. It was the least they could do.

In his mind, it was over. In all honesty, he should never have allowed it to get this far, should have done something before now. But it was difficult. After all, it was his father, and that made a huge difference. He imagined almost every being on the planet would struggle to go up against their dad at such a young age. But the time was at hand, and there could be no sympathy, no regrets, no hesitation. It had to be done, for his sake, his mother and brother's sakes and of course for the good of the community as a whole. And so with absolutely no remorse, he called on his magic, hoping that it would be the last time he'd use it in anger. Fate just laughed, thinking that there's wasn't a chance in hell of that happening.

Through the haze of fiction and reality blurring into one, Marg did not know what he was doing. Unable to use his magic to heal any of his internal wounds because of the state of his mind, instinctively he did the only thing he could. He lashed out at his attacker, with everything he had.

Facing his son, expecting some sort of all out attack, he was momentarily caught off guard as the sensation of magic sprang into life behind him. Reacting with just the human senses that had been part of him for so long now, he dived off to his left, ducked into a roll and leapt up onto his feet, all in one long, swift move.

About to fry his father like a sausage on a barbecue, Man froze at the sight of brilliant, fluorescent green magic crackling into life just in front of Marg. Before he'd even had time to think, 'What the...?', wicked tendrils of poisonous, green, supernatural energy splintered out of the naga's wavering hand, carving open the air molecules between him and his father. But that wasn't the biggest surprise. That would have to have been reserved for the cat-like reactions of his father, diving and rolling out of the way, edging his way to safety. At that exact moment, Man realised the trouble he was in, facing the full force of what was left of the naga's wrath.

During the course of their limited training, they'd covered shields, but not in much detail, having only spent an hour or two practicing. Marg had decided that was enough, and that their time was better spent training on how to use offensive magic. And so here Man was, about to be inundated with spiteful, poisonous power, intent on revenge and killing, not at all meant for him of course, but still presenting him with a predicament and one he only had a moment to decide what to do.

All they'd seen from behind Man's hulking great body was a flash of bright, brilliant green light, and then their deluded, deadly leader diving out of the way, off to the right as they looked at it. Still holding each other tight, they both wondered what the hell was going on.

With no other thoughts or plans and deflecting away the oncoming threat with magic not an option, the elder of the two brothers followed in his father's footsteps and decided to get out of the way of certain doom. Knees already bent, he pushed off, and with one flap of his mighty wings, had taken fully to the air, out of any immediate danger, although that's not what that tiny voice, the one that only made an appearance when everything felt wrong, screamed.

Off to one side, the leader, back on his feet, watched in total admiration, tinged with more than a little jealousy, as his son pounced skyward, or in this case, ceilingward. Memories of times gone past flooded his mind; immediately though his attention was drawn back to the here and now, a sliver of a smile breaking out across his harsh features.

'Oh dear,' he thought. 'I don't think they've accounted for that.'

Huddled together, mother and son were absolutely dumbstruck to find a shocking, spider web array of fluorescent green projectiles heading directly for them as Man lifted off into the air and out of the way. Frozen solid with fear, their mother's thoughts were only with her sons, glad that one had got to relative safety, scared for the other, knowing that he didn't have the courage or the convictions of his sibling. In an act enabled only by a mother's love, she grabbed Josh's hand tight, and as she mouthed the words, "I love you," she jumped in front of her son, holding him tight.

Doubling back on himself in the tightest of turns, only then did he realise exactly what had happened and how, by avoiding the attack, he'd put those he loved in the way of danger. Helplessly, Man watched as the magical cascade of poisonous missiles closed in on Josh and their mother. One thing was certain, they didn't stand a chance. And then, quick as a flash, she sacrificed everything, throwing herself in front of her youngest son, a self sacrifice she was only too willing to make for her offspring, a mother's duty fulfilled, forgoing everything she'd ever known for love and the chance for her children to have a better life.

Off to one side, still smirking, counting himself lucky to be alive, the leader watched the wicked naga magic meant for him slam into the back of his children's mother, infiltrating her with an array of toxins, causing her skin to blacken and harden, eliciting a high-pitched scream that cut through everything around them. With all the poisonous darts having either hit the icy walls, or been absorbed by the self sacrificing mother, a decision was made, one that reeked of havoc, vengeance and fury.

Man dropped like a stone out of the air directly in front of his father, his face a twisted grimace full of rage, thoughts of revenge consuming him fully.

Shocked at not having more time, the leader took one step back, trying to assess his situation. It wasn't good, that was for sure.

One thought, and one thought only, made him open his mouth. Right at this very moment, he knew that his life depended on him appearing to care for another. A brand new experience for him, he gave his all in his pretence.

"Oh my God... what's happened?" he voiced, shaking like a tree in the wind.

"DON'T YOU DARE GIVE ME THAT!" roared the dragon form of his son, stomping closer.

"She's hurt, she's hurt... we have to save her."

Still Man closed in, brilliant, bright yellow and orange swirls of flame washing around inside his mouth, tiny sparks washing out through the miniscule gaps between his teeth.

"I'M GOING TO RIP YOUR HEAD OFF AND PEE DOWN YOUR NECK," Man bellowed furiously, closing to almost within striking distance.

Here it came... the single biggest lie of his life, and one that he hoped would keep him in the land of the living.

"I can save her... it's still possible. But we have to hurry."

That stopped the hulking great prehistoric form in its tracks instantly. But would it be enough?

Collapsing in his arms, Josh watched wide-eyed as blood spilled from between his mother's lips and dribbled precariously down her chin.

"NO!" he pleaded.

But as she slipped through his arms and slammed to the ground, a distinctive green aura enveloped her, as crusty, black patches of withered skin started to appear across her body.

"MAN... HELP! She's dying, we have to save her, we have to do something!"

His brother's voice ringing in his ears from behind him, Man knew better than to turn around and present his back to his father.

"I can save her," repeated the leader, "but there's little time. It has to be done quickly."

"THEN DO IT!" Man demanded, stepping off to one side.

Here it comes... the gamble that might or might not save not only his life, but that of the planet as well.

"If I'm going to do just that... I need something in return."

Man was incredulous, although knowing his father he really shouldn't have been.

"You want to bargain at a time like this, when you yourself have stated that time is of the essence?" he ranted, his voice quivering with fury, about to blow his top.

"I'm not going to save her only to find that you try and kill me. What would be the point of that?"

Desperate, and barely able to believe a word his father said, out of the corner of his eye, he could just make out his mother lying on the ground, tossing and turning, looking in as much pain as he'd ever seen another being. Pain from the sight of this forced his thinking to become clear, knowing that if he wanted to save his mother, there was only one thing to do... agree to any and all demands his father had.

"What is it you want?"

"I'm going to say a sentence, and you're going to repeat it."

"And what's the catch?"

"It's a magical declaration, one that will stop you from killing me. If you say it with your willpower and magic behind it, then you'll be no threat to me, and I can gladly save your mother."

"But it's no guarantee that you won't kill me, is that right?"

"It doesn't work both ways... no."

'Of all the things...' Man thought. 'If I agree to it, then I can't kill him. How will he be stopped? But if I don't agree and quickly, Mother dies... this is unbelievable!'

Of course there really was only one choice and both beings knew it. There was only ever going to be one outcome, that's how much Man loved his mother.

"Let's do it, and quickly. And by the way, if you fail to save her... I'll find a way, on that you have my word."

Nodding his head, the leader understood the threat to his life. Delving deep into his vast repository of magical knowledge, he trawled the very dark depths before finally coming up with the information he needed.

"You need to repeat after me exactly, as well as adding a significant amount of your willpower and magic. If you don't, I'll know."

Nodding in understanding, Man closed his huge eyelids, and waited for it to begin, dreading the consequences of what he was about to do, all the time fearful for his mother's life.

"Et ego vos moneo acquiesco, et venientes ad pedes vestri, ita ut colonus erit usque ad finem dierum," the leader stated carefully, sure to pronounce every word correctly.

Swallowing nervously, Man flooded himself with magic, mustered up all the willpower he could under the circumstances, and repeated every word, still not entirely sure to what he was agreeing.

"Et ego vos moneo acquiesco, et venientes ad pedes vestri, ita ut colonus erit usque ad finem dierum."

In effect what he'd done was bind himself magically to an agreement that, when translated, went something like this.

"I acquiesce and proffer myself at your feet, agreeing to serve you until the end of days."

As the last word rolled off Man's tongue, an uncomfortable tingling sensation, starting at the talons on his feet, spreading to his head and encompassing his arms and the rest of his body, pricked his skin and boiled his blood. Magic molecules collided within him, wrapping around his very core, bonding him to his word. It felt as though at the back of his mind, a very different type of morality sat their waiting to override any of his decisions. Unusual, ancient magic working in the background was how best to describe it.

Back in the present, already regretting his decision, he turned to face his father.

"Save her," he implored.

"I can't do that."

"WHAT!" barked Man.

"But I can show you how to."

"Go on."

Deep inside the leader, he savoured the moment in all its deliciousness. It was truly his crowning glory, both magnificent in its timing and fantastic in the turnaround that it had presented over the course of a few minutes. Fate, as he well knew, could be a fickle mistress, but on this occasion, here and now, had acted more like a benevolent god towards him. Determined not to squander the chance, he ploughed on.

"To save her, you have to neutralise the poison seeping

through her body. There's only one way to do that...
FIRE!"

"WHAT! YOU'RE KIDDING!"

"No. I'm telling you how to save her. You have to run your flame across the whole of her body, keeping it at a very steady temperature. If done correctly, the poison will burn off and slowly start to seep and evaporate out of her. It has to be constant, and probably at the lowest temperature you can maintain. Three or four long slow passes should do the trick. I wouldn't wait much longer if I were you, otherwise it will be too late."

At that precise point in his very short lived life, his father's suggestion seemed like the absolute definition of insanity. But what other choice did he have? Reaching out telepathically, hoping not to gain any sort of attention, he tapped into his brother's mind and told him what his father had said, waiting to hear his opinion.

"If he says that'll work, I'm sure it will."

"But does it sound right?" asked Man, confused conflicted and running out of time.

"Why wouldn't it?" replied Josh.

"Think, dammit, think, Josh! Although our magical knowledge maybe limited, we've learnt the basics over the last year or so. Nothing like this, I have to admit, but our studies have included the sciences. What he suggests sounds to me as though it couldn't possibly work. Think about it as a whole, disregard the magical aspects if you like. Could it, or should it work? Tell me your opinion."

Under more pressure than he'd ever been in his entire life, the younger brother thought about his sibling's question, trying to remember all the work he'd done in class, trying to remember things he'd not even learnt yet. Try as he might though, the answers he was searching for just wouldn't come. That is, until he received an almost imperceptible magical nudge that tipped him over the edge.

"It's right," he uttered across their link for only Man to

hear.

"Are you sure?" asked his brother.

"I am," he replied confidently.

A smile of epic proportions spread out across the leader's mind, not making a dent in his stoic physical face.

Stomping straight over to his mother's green and black form, his heart almost broken, everything about this felt... WRONG! With a capital W. But nothing about the last few minutes made sense, from the smouldering naga corpse on the icy, white floor, to his father ordering his thugs to kill his mother, to this. It was inexplicable, unimaginable, the very worst nightmare possible. Stuck in an unfathomable position, he did the only thing he could... he trusted those around him, his brother and, unfortunately, his father. And so, leaning over his mother, he tapped into all his supernatural power and brought forth the lightest, least dense, purest form of flame that he'd known, and very slowly started washing it along his mother's prone form.

Instantly she cried out, screaming in absolute agony, his efforts appearing to make things much worse.

"DON'T STOP!" yelled his father over the cacophony. "IT'S THE ONLY WAY TO SAVE HER!"

Reluctantly, and being torn apart by his mother's abject misery, he continued to subject her to the flame, watching as undamaged parts of her skin turned to charcoal, as pockets of poison bubbled and popped. It broke his heart. It was supposed to.

From close by, Josh watched his brother, willing him on, briefly wondering what he was doing, having no memory of their conversation.

'Odd,' he thought, 'that Man has chosen to do that to her. It doesn't seem right.'

A short way away, Marg received the lightest telepathic touch, almost as if a search party was trying to contact him. In his weakened and delirious state, all he could do was respond in kind, something that would have huge ramifications not only for his race, but for the planet at large. The dragon leader looked on, taking it all in, knowing that his plan was about to come to fruition, with nothing able to stop it now.

Arching her back, the boy's mother let out a horrific scream that seemed to last forever, much to her son's dismay. That nightmarish, out of control, something is totally and utterly wrong feeling that Man had felt from the offset exploded inside him. Against his better judgement, he stopped what he was doing, and turned his giant prehistoric head back over his shoulder to look straight at his father. Taking in the self satisfied smirk that now emboldened his face turned Man's insides colder than the chamber they now found themselves in. Flame nowhere to be seen, he took a step forward towards his mother, ready to flood her with all the magic he had, having absolutely no idea if that would do anything at all. Healing magic hadn't been dealt with over the course of his very incomplete training, and so he had no idea whether he could do it or not, or even if it was a possibility.

It was then that it happened, and his world changed forever in an instant. A chain knock-on-effect caused by the flame heating the poison reached a critical point deep within her broken body. Atoms merged as a catastrophic chain reaction that could no longer be stopped took over. Out of nowhere, her left leg exploded, chunks of flesh and muscle flying up into the air.

"NO!" screamed Man, remorsefully, making a beeline for the rest of her body.

It was a good job he was in his dragon guise, otherwise it might just have been the end of his short life.

Two simultaneous explosions, one in the middle of her chest cavity, one smack bang in the centre of her forehead, knocked him back off his feet, no small feat in itself. All that remained of the woman loved unconditionally by the two young boys that had never known anything else was a pile of poisonous goo, spread across quite a wide area. As toxic steam from the remains started to fill the room, the reality of the situation began to sink in. Josh dropped to his knees, tears freezing his eyes open, sniffling and sobbing, desperate to once again see his mother. Across the way, the boy's father maintained his well practised smirk, standing stoically still, waiting to see how this would play out, confident because of the binding agreement that he'd forged beforehand that no harm could befall him. That only left Man, who was only now realising what had just happened. His father had tricked him into killing his mother in the most painful way possible. A righteous fury and anger the likes of which the world had rarely seen erupted throughout every molecule of his body, boiling his blood, stoking his rage, priming him ready for revenge. Magic ebbed and flowed, fired and flared, filling his body from head to tail. But that wasn't all that happened, as those around him could bear witness to. The crystalline structures that covered his body started to retract and disappear, forcing him to cry out in pain.

Looking on in disbelief, it was at this point that the leader started to become worried, not liking anything he didn't understand or have control over. And truth be told, he, just like everyone else, had absolutely no clue as to what was going on.

"Aaaarrrrggghhhh!" cried out Man as scales and blood ripped from his body in the aftermath of the crystal spikes disappearing out of nowhere. Tortured by physical pain and pounded by the psychological pain of having caused his mother's death only moments before, his huge dinosaur-like body crumpled to the floor, wings outstretched, the whole cavern shaking like an earthquake had just hit nearby. The booming sound was monstrous, as the leader was tossed back off his feet. Josh was thrown across the room, smacking his head into the wall. Their mother's remains scattered, merging with the surrounding ice and rock. The concussion wave from the impact was enough to end Marg's life, his serpent-like body thrown up in the air, before crashing down unceremoniously. As the cavern continued to shake, and screaming in the far distance assaulted their ears, magic ignited another change deep within the dragon form of the boy who'd just lost his mother.

Whether through magic, love, betrayal, revenge, anger, rage, loss or a combination of them all, a cold, calculating darkness spread out from the tips of Man's wings, slowly encompassing his entire body, changing his colour from fantastic shades of brilliant blue, to one all-embodying shade of matt black. It was staggering, unreal, and as frightful as you could imagine. And his outer colour wasn't the only thing affected. Deep inside, at the core of his very being, where his magic resided, the supernatural power itself was influenced. It too had become corrupted, as that's what had happened, and it too changed colour, from blistering shades of blue, green, red, purple, yellow and orange, it was now just a dark, dull black, still flaming away, now a menacing source of unpredictable evil.

After thirty seconds or so, the rumbling of the surroundings stopped, and the humungous, matt black dragon stirred.

Josh still lay unconscious at the far end of the cavern, their naga guest curled up, dead not far away. Aside from the deceased thugs, that just left Man and his father, the leader, now gathering up his magic, astounded at the turn of events and not sure what to make of anything.

As his son stumbled to his feet, outstretched black wings helping him with his balance, the leader knew that the time had come.

"You will desist and obey me now!" he ordered, flooding his words with just a sprinkle of magic.

Rising up on his feet, looking down at the insignificant form of his father barking out orders, a righteous fury, at least that's how it felt, rushed up inside him. With the binding agreement at the back of his mind, something felt different deep down inside him. Rolling his monstrous jaw, squirting out flame this way and that, finally he turned in his father's direction, intent on having his revenge. Plodding forward despite the orders to the contrary, he smiled as the sudden discomfort appeared on the leader's face.

'So the magical binding doesn't work after all,' he thought as he whipped around in a three hundred and sixty degree arc, his tail brushing his father's legs away from under him, causing him to crash to the floor, knocking the wind right out of him.

Full on panic at the thought of being killed rushing through him, the leader, prone on the floor, raised both hands and fired a rapid series of fireballs in the gigantic black dragon's direction. Man didn't move a muscle, just standing there, letting the ancient magic bounce off him.

'It tickles,' he thought, as yet another fireball scorched his belly.

Terrified beyond belief, believing death to be only a moment or so away, the leader resorted to the worst magic he knew, giving everything, putting all his willpower behind the effort to kill his son, using up every last drop of power he had.

A sizzling bolt of ethereal green lightning sliced through one of his wing membranes, causing him to cry out in agony, catching him off guard. It was enough however, to detach him from thoughts of his mother, startling him back to the present, refocusing his mind on making his father pay for what he'd done. And so without further ado, he attacked as he'd been shown how by Marg, and with the full force of his dark magic behind it, let rip with a shower of flaming projectiles.

Power spent, he watched in horror as magical mayhem headed his way from the outstretched hand of his son. This was it, what a way to go. But as the supernatural power approached, getting within only a matter of inches from his face, unbelievably, one by one, the projectiles puffed out of existence. It was hard to tell who was the more surprised... the leader, or his son. Both looked on in utter disbelief. In a frenzied fit of anger, Man launched yet another barrage, this time with as much magic and power behind it as his body would allow. The exact same thing happened. More than a little cocky now, the leader rose to his feet, a harsh laughter echoing from his mouth. This just enraged Man even more. With more speed than either of them would have thought possible, the giant dragon form whirled around one hundred and eighty degrees, and with the talons on his feet, kicked the leader straight in the face, sending him ten metres into the air, smashing into one of the side walls. Hitting with a THUMP, before sliding comically down the wall, the young boy dragon was sure that he had inflicted massive amounts of pain. And he'd been right. Broken ribs, a shattered knee cap and three long bleeding gashes across his face from the raking talons was enough to have the leader doubled over in distress. Immediately, Man moved in to finish things off, knowing that one more strike now would surely be enough. Hovering over the pathetic little form, the youngster lifted up one of his massive legs, with a view to bringing it down atop his father, finishing him off once and for all. But with his leg wavering in the air, there was simply nothing he could do about bringing it down, despite putting all his will and focus behind it.

From the ground, another taunting laugh echoed, this time accompanied by a few well chosen words.

"Hahaha... it appears that the magic worked to some degree. You can inflict a reasonable amount of pain, but it won't let you kill me. How funny is that?"

Now even angrier, Man tried again, putting the full force of everything he had into bringing down his leg and crushing the life out of his father... NOTHING! Frustrated beyond belief, another course of action presented itself. Searching his enormous belly for the tiniest spark of magic, he found it instantly. Commanding it to do his bidding, the spark turned into a roaring fire, which instantly started to make a break for it. As the confines of his throat tried to expand, due to the size of the fireball heading at speed towards his mouth, his mighty jaws opened of their own accord, pointing in the direction of his father. Pleased with the solution he'd developed, he savoured every second, looking forward to the giant ball of flame warming his teeth on its way to incinerate the one being on the planet he hated the most. As the swirling mass of heat and flame exited his throat, into his mouth, the warmth and flame died out with the faintest of puffs, leaving smoky residue lingering in and around his tongue.

'NO!' he thought, slapping his wings together in frustration.

"I'm sorry son," echoed a voice, catching his attention, "but you just can't do it. The magic won't let you."

In that instant, he knew his father was right and that any chance he'd ever had of killing him was gone forever.

Despite the leader's injuries and the acute pain he was feeling, he was very much the dragon of old, full of cunning and always thinking, noting that Man had absolutely nothing in the way of a mental defence blocking any kind of attack. And so with that in mind, he used the same trick he had on the boy's brother, but instead of planting a memory he subliminally planted a couple of ideas, ones that were yet to bubble to the surface, but should with just a little encouragement. This particular approach wouldn't work on most dragons, but Man and his brother were particularly naive and had no real world experience, unlike their father. In essence, the youngster had absolutely no chance, not even able to recognise the attack, let alone defend against it.

The first idea was that the nagas were fully responsible for the death of his mother... not too much of a leap given the poisonous projectiles that had killed her had originated from one of their own. Vengeance and wrath should be brought to bear against them, no matter what.

The second was that the dragons and their domain had

a huge part to play, not only in his mother's death, but in all of their suffering. After all, they'd been confined here by them, all that time ago, left to endure the absurdly low temperatures, left to die a shameful death with no chance of redemption. Again, it wasn't much of a stretch, but these subconscious suggestions, tempered with just a touch of magic, should infest every living part of Man, driving him on to deadlier deeds, giving him that edge that his father knew was missing from the boy.

Rising unsteadily to his feet, brushing off the ice, the leader winced as he stretched, turning to face his son, hoping that his little deception had started to take root.

"Join me, son. Together we can work out a way to leave this place, visit a whole world of pain on the rest of his race," he said, nodding in the direction of Marg's corpse, "have our revenge on the dragon domain, given what they've done to us all, and finally take our rightful place in the world order, at the top table, so to speak."

Conflicting emotions ran riot throughout Man's huge dragon body. When his father had nodded towards the naga cadaver on the floor, his first thoughts were of sorrow and pain. Suddenly though, bubbling up from nowhere, a dark, crashing wave of resentment, bitterness and hatred washed over him, allowing him to contemplate disgraceful, deadly deeds. As the seconds passed, his mind relished those thoughts... revenge, redemption, retribution... it all made perfect sense, at least to him anyway. In that moment, every last part of him had gone dark... his body, his magic, his character. There would be no coming back from this... EVER!

Echoes from the memories of what had happened over the last few minutes faded in and out of his mind, causing sorrow and pain, anger and rage. A few of the things stood out more than others. Of course his mother's agonising death, but one other thing as well... his brother's acknowledgement that he was doing the right thing by trying to cure her with his flame. That had spurred him on, tipped him over the edge. Had it just been his father's voice saying so, he'd have never done it, never believed it to be right. But Josh's verification that he was doing the right thing had been enough to spur him on. And so it was, there and then, that he made a conscious decision, one that would see the sibling's relationship change forever.

"I'll join you in your quest," stated Man. "But there are conditions."

"Really?" replied the leader.

"Yes."

"I don't doubt they could be accommodated."

Man nodded his head.

"We need to get started. I can sense that they're almost here. Undoubtedly you'll have to get your hands dirty. Are you up for that?"

"I've already agreed haven't I? My word should be enough for you."

Sensing that the magic had well and truly taken over, and not even an inkling of deception from his son, the leader smiled, his first true smile for a very long time, knowing that this would be the start of something very special, and that sometime in the future, together, they could look forward to ruling the world. Father and son, governing the planet side by side... didn't that sound good.

Two hours later, they arrived, unceremoniously shooting up out of the stream, close to the dragon prisoner, a cadre of bodyguards first, swiftly followed by a magnificent looking monster of a naga, dripping wet, a keen intelligence clearly visible behind both vertically-slit pupils. Obviously no ordinary specimen, he looked regal and majestic, the very tip of his tail the darkest blue possible, whilst in concentric circles moving upwards, the scales of his body gradually lightened until the palest sky blue beset his head and ever moving gills. Marg's monarch had arrived, and although he wasn't there to greet him, a party from the stranded dragon colony was

Man stood silently beside his father, a swirling mass of emotion, cloaked in his human form, trying to remain as neutral as possible, shielding his mind from any sort of probe or query, in case they attempted to get to the truth. Deep down, he felt alive, invigorated and ready to dish out redemption when the time should come. But he knew that it wasn't now, not least because they could all easily slip back into the stream and disappear out of sight, never to be seen again. Following the plan remained the best bet he knew, so for the moment he would go along with his father, at least until the appropriate opportunity presented itself.

Aware of the conflict inside his son, the leader hoped to hell he'd hold everything in place, at least until they were far away from the stream. After that, he could have the revenge he thought he sought, that would prove to be just desserts for both the nagas and the wicked boy. Until then, he had to be diplomatic, and starting now, he would be.

"Greetings, gentle beings," he announced, stepping forward towards the legion of nagas that made up a wall directly in front of him. "I am the leader of this small colony. I assume Marg told you all about us."

"Weeeee reeeeeceeiived hiiiisss meeessssaggge," announced the most stunning of them all, the wall in front of him parting as he did so.

'Odd,' thought all of the dragons simultaneously. 'Why on earth does he talk like that?'

'It doesn't matter,' thought the leader to himself. 'Soon, he'll have plenty of time to work on his pronunciation.'

"That's great," observed the leader, thrusting out his hand.

Slowly, the naga clearly in charge, much to the disappointment of all the others, slid gracefully up to Man's father, and very gently grasped his hand and shook it.

'Petty weaklings,' was the leader's first thought, still smiling diplomatically.

Man had to force himself not to throw up.

"Caaaannn I asssk whhheerree issss ouuurrr brrroootheeerr?"

Quick as a flash, the leader responded, not a hint of betrayal evident.

"He's resting, your highness. Would you like us to take you to him?"

"Thhhaaat wouuuld beeee pruuuudeeent."

"If you'd like to follow me."

Turning, the leader started to pace off in the direction of the remote enclave, his plan to get the group of them far from the stream's entrance looking as though it had worked.

Before he had a chance to take another step, the naga monarch twisted his upper body around to face two of the other guards.

"Staaaay heeereee," he ordered.

Bowing the top halves of their snake-like bodies in obedience, the naga king turned and started to slither along in time with the dragon leader's silent footsteps.

Before they'd travelled even a metre, their honoured guest stopped, looking over across to his right up onto a small raised ridge.

"Whaaaat isssss thaaaatt?" he asked curiously.

"Ahhh," reflected their leader, playing up to the crowd. "That, your majesty, is one of our dragon captors who was trapped here when the explosives were ignited and blew the entrance out. He's been our guest for as long as we've been here."

"I seeeeeee," murmured the naga monarch thoughtfully.

"Why isssss heeee iiiin thaaat staaaatee?"

"He suffers regularly from delusions, still thinking that he resides back in the dragon domain with his friends and family. We've made him as comfortable as we can, but as you can imagine, he still presents a clear and present danger. We care for him, share our food with him, even try to counsel him, but during the course of time, none of it has done any good. He's still prone to violent outbursts, still self harms, still his temper can change in the blink of an eye. One moment he's quiet, sedate and sane, the next he can be thrashing about, cursing blue murder, trying to wreck the place. In all honesty, we don't know what to do. With our magic contained by the cold, we have exhausted all possibilities. If you know of any other solution, we'd welcome your input. All we want is for him to be well and live out a happy and productive life with us."

Oh how the lies slip so easily off the tongue.

"I wiiiillll haaaaveee a thiiiiiiink. Maaaybee theeere's soomethiiiiiing weee caaan dooo."

Striding away, the leader nodded, a smile flickering across his face as he would have expected it to do.

As Man fell in time with the two of them, the squad of nagas slithering up behind them all, the naga monarch introduced himself.

"Yooooouuuu maaaaay caaaaallllll meeee Vasuki," he just about managed to get out, the words seeming to cause him a great deal of difficulty.

"This is my son, Man," the leader said proudly, clapping the young man on the shoulder. And you can refer to me as..."

As they disappeared behind the rock wall, the noise carried off in the breeze.

During the course of their journey, the leader showed them the magical hydroponic bays, announcing that only their best fruit and vegetables would be on show later for a feast to be held in their honour. The naga king seemed suitably impressed and flattered, as you would imagine. Across all of this, examples of just how hard they had to work to survive, and the drudgery of their population's daily life was explained in graphic detail. From the expression on the king's face, he was buying it all, hook, line and sinker. From there, the conversation moved on to their betrayal by the rest of the dragon domain, offering up the exact same account that he had to Marg, all those days ago. Of course he threw in some emotion, righteous anger, fury, sorrow and of course a deep held belief that he had to overturn a dastardly wrong that was somehow playing out right at this very minute, across the planet as a whole. Not only did their monarch believe it by the time he finished, but so did the bodyguards, to a being. It was a masterclass in deception, one any spy would have felt lucky to attend.

Only moments from the remote enclave now, the nagas, distracted by the tale of fiction so passionately told by the leader, had neither noticed, or had chosen to subconsciously ignore, a build up of human shapes following in their wake. Given what was about to happen, that would prove costly.

Turning a sharp corner beneath an icy overhang, the large contingent of beings opened out into the cavern that less than three hours ago had staged the mother of all battles (mother... get it again?!).

As all the nagas piled in, the human shapes behind them crowded around the exit, preventing their escape.

With the frozen cadaver of Marg the stunning centrepiece, the king turned to the leader of the outcast dragons.

"Whaaaat issss theeee meaaaaaaaning oofff thiiiisss?"

Arms raised in triumph, turning three hundred and sixty degrees, the leader stepped out in front of everybody, relishing the spotlight, soaking up every last ounce of what was going on.

"The meaning, as you so politely put it, is that you're all our prisoners, and you shall remain so until we've run out of demands."

"Yoooouuuur'eee kiiiiddding!" replied the naga king, flustered and completely off guard.

"I'm afraid not," declared the leader, more than a hint of menace ringing through his voice.

Deep within his mind, Vasuki gave the order to all his guards. No second rate, stranded, encumbered by the cold dragons would ever hold him hostage! Little did he know.

As one, the nagas sprang into action, igniting their unusual supernatural power, ready to give their all to save their monarch. Unfortunately for them, the dragon leader had already dished out his orders, and in a battle where who had the least scruples was probably going to win, in only a matter of moments they realised that losing was a very real prospect.

Three nagas were taken out instantaneously from behind, before things had even kicked off, by Man's father's second in command and his two sidekicks that both had their magic returned to them. Simultaneously, a writhing mass of human shapes inundated the remaining nagas, scrambling over their tails, scaling their wriggling bodies, piercing their gills with needle sharp stalactites, listening in satisfaction as the painful gurgles echoed around the cavern. During all the mayhem and chaos a shimmering human shape had started to transform... MAN! Seemingly out of nowhere, a huge, matt black, prehistoric dragon, roaring cones of flame, shooting swelteringly hot balls of majestic fire indiscriminately into the crowd of overwhelmed nagas appeared, scaring the living hell out of the enemy's fighting force. In their lives, they'd never seen anything like it.

Interrupting Man's vicious killing spree, a voice abruptly echoed around his mind.

"Calm yourself. We need three or four of them, plus their king, alive if our plan is to have any chance of succeeding."

It was just about enough to put the brakes on things as far as he was concerned, the bigger picture of the price he would exact on the dragon domain, almost enough to focus on. And so, smashing their king to the ground, just as he'd started to unleash some kind of bright pink energy from the tips of his fingers, Man stomped one huge foot across his chest, and pinned him in place with his razor sharp talons. Seeing their monarch captured and defeated, the rest of the nagas gave in, some losing their lives, others captured, on a day that would be remembered in the annals of history as the start of the beginning of the end of the world.

A few hours later, the start of the plan proper had been enacted. One of the nagas had been released, and told to find the rest of his kind with their demands. Sheepishly he'd licked his wounds and gone head first into the icy cold stream without hesitation, having fully memorised the dragon outcasts' requirements for his monarch's release. These included a way back to the mainland around the equator, heat, clothes, supplies, food, and a whole host of magical knowledge, including some of the most closely guarded supernatural naga secrets, in particular, some that the leader had stumbled upon on when breaking through Marg's mind. Oddly, one of the demands was for ten sets of chains, and not just any chains, but ones used strictly to control outcasts and criminals, not that there were many of those in the ancient race's society. Again something scavenged from Marg's mind, they looked as though they'd do the job in restraining and containing not only the desperate dragon guard that had been here all those decades, but the naga king for the time being. And having spare sets wouldn't hurt, after all, who knew what other potential prisoners they just might encounter? In all it was a successful negotiation, I say negotiation, in essence it was nothing of the sort. The demands were to be met otherwise their king died the most painful death.

In the remote enclave, the naga monarch, surrounded by Man and two of the other dragon magic wielders, sat up against the far wall, having been told what the

155

consequences would be of any attempt to escape or contact his race. So far he'd complied, but he did so only under duress and the thoughts of what would happen to those of his kin here left alive. He had no idea how many that was, but he knew some were still living and breathing, and since they'd pledged their lives to him all that time ago, and served him without thought up until now, that was the least he could do. Little did he know that his actions here and now, would cost his kind more than ever, possibly destroying everything he'd ever known.

As the days turned into weeks, demands were met. A permanent guard was stationed by the edge of the stream, constantly on the lookout for an encroachment by the nagas, ready to repel a rescue attempt at a moment's notice. Through the use of the nagas' ancient and unusual power, the confines of the encampment were finally heated, allowing all the remaining dragon residents access to their magical powers, thus making their force stronger, and the naga king's position weaker. Food and clothes were procured; magic was either shared or taken forcefully. When the chains finally arrived, the dragon guard formerly known as Unlucky was strung up first. Jeered and cheered by onlookers as the strength and magic sapping restraints took effect, over the course of the last few weeks, he'd barely been fed and now looked like a 'Bag O Bones', a name that captured the imagination and stuck. Along the frozen wall from him, the naga king was acquainted with the chains, much to his disgust and surprise. The leader thought this deliciously ironic, something that pleased him greatly. As all this took shape, and efforts to get them back to the mainland around the equator were put into effect, father and son met up late one night to make good on the conditions that Man had stipulated in return for his help.

"Are you sure about this?" asked the leader, knowing that there was no going back. "Although I fully understand, it's a cruel and very permanent thing to do."

"You've taught us our history... I want it done. It's

nothing more than he deserves."

Nodding, the leader continued walking alongside his son, the one with the deluge of power and magic, not the halfwit outcast with which he had little truck.

"If that's your decision, then it will be made so, as long as you realise the consequences."

"I do," uttered Man, his mind elsewhere, somewhere back where he considered the betrayal to have begun.

Rounding a corner, they approached the wall where the prisoners had been restrained by the magical chains, not far from the edge of the ever gurgling stream.

There, kicking and beating the weathered old dragon with a huge chunk of metal, was Josh, his hair filthy and dank, still dressed in his ragged scraps of cloth, looking much the worse for wear. Immediately on seeing his father and brother, he stopped, almost standing to attention.

"I see you've developed a playful side," quipped his father.

Nobody laughed. After a short, awkward silence, his father once again spoke. All the time Josh's pain ridden eyes pleaded with his brother, to be given one last chance. Man just looked on in disgust, barely even registering his brother's presence.

"A decision has been made," announced the leader between the three of them.

Man just looked stoically on. Josh's hands shook uncontrollably. Addressing Josh, his father continued.

"As you know, any form of betrayal, no matter how small, cannot be tolerated in dragon society. Normally if such a thing is proved, that particular individual is either cast out, or in some cases is sentenced to the death penalty."

A tiny whine of fear squeaked out from between Josh's lips. The leader continued.

"With what's happened here, both could apply."

Silence, apart from the grumbling of the stream surrounded all of them.

"Leniency though, has been applied," their father continued. "From here on in, you shall be commanded to stay here and guard the prisoners as though your life depended upon it. Do you understand?"

Josh nodded fervently.

"As well, as an added deterrent for anyone else, you shall suffer one of the most disdainful and embarrassing fates of all dragons. Your name will be changed to add in the 'IM' suffix that over the course of time has come to signify that of a traitor or a dragon who can't be trusted. From now until the end of your days, you will be known as JOSHIM, and you will only answer to that. Have I made myself clear?"

"Yes," squeaked Josh, grateful not to be receiving the death penalty.

"Our business here is concluded. You will watch over these two until you are ordered to do otherwise. At some point in the future, others may join them. Make sure you are ready."

"I will, I will."

Turning away without looking back, both the leader and his son stalked the edge of the wall before cutting back along the other side of it and headed for their chambers, eager to feel the newfound warmth they offered.

"You know I love you Man, son," prompted his father, Troydenn.

"I know. I love you too Father."

I hope you've enjoyed reading the story of evil personified. If you'd like to see how it fits in to the greater good of the main series of books, why not pick up A Threat From The Past and start your rollercoaster journey into a world of fresh, original Young Adult Fantasy.

OTHER BOOKS IN THE SERIES:
A Threat from the Past
A Chilling Revelation
A Twisted Prophecy
Earth's Custodians
A Fiery Farewell (coming soon)

ABOUT THE AUTHOR
Paul Cude is a husband, father, field hockey player and aspiring photographer. Lost without his hockey stick, he can often be found in between writing and chauffeuring children, reading anything from comics to sci-fi, fantasy to thrillers. Too often found chained to his computer, it would be little surprise to find him, in his free time, somewhere on the Dorset coastline, chasing over rocks and sand in an effort to capture his wonderful wife and lovely kids with his camera. Paul Cude is also the author of the Bentwhistle the Dragon series of books.

Thank you for reading.....

If you could take a couple of moments to write a review, it would be much appreciated.

CONNECT WITH PAUL ONLINE:
www.paulcude.com
Twitter: @paul_cude
Facebook: Paul Cude
Instagram: paulcude

Printed in Poland
by Amazon Fulfillment
Poland Sp. z o.o., Wrocław